PIERRE BOULEZ
CONVERSATIONS WITH CÉLES

PIERRE BOULEZ

conversations with
Célestin Deliège

Foreword by Robert Wangermée

EULENBURG BOOKS
LONDON

First published in French under the title
*Par Volonté et par Hasard: Entretiens avec
Célestin Deliège.*
© 1975, Les Editions du Seuil, Paris.
English translation © 1976, Ernst Eulenburg Ltd.
ISBN 0 903873 21 4 (hardback)
0 903873 22 2 (paperback)
Printed and bound in England by
Caligraving Ltd, Thetford, Norfolk.

CONTENTS

FOREWORD

Pierre Boulez has written a lot about music. Before a new work, or while actually composing it, he has often published both polemical and theoretical texts: polemical when he violently criticised composers whose example he wished to reject, the better to pursue his own ideas; and theoretical when he tried to justify in advance the direction he was giving to his creative work. For the past twelve years or so, however, Boulez has been more discreet.

The prime interest of his conversations with Célestin Deliège (which were recorded in 1972 for a series of broadcasts by Radio-diffusion-Télévision Belge, and completed in the summer of 1974) is that they renew our contact with Boulez, his ideas and his enthusiasms, after a period in which — although addressing himself to a wider public — it has been above all as a conductor that he has fought for the music he loves.

From the Sonatina for flute and piano to . . . *explosante-fixe* . . ., it is his works that shape the chapters of these conversations: Deliège gets Boulez to explain each of them, to describe their origins, and comment on them. However, this is no mere chronicle. First of all, Boulez is very lucidly critical of himself; if he explains the train of thought which led him to write *Polyphonie X*, he can take an objective attitude towards the rigid organisation he adopted at that time and it is the occasion for this reputedly over-'mathematical' musician to maintain that technique should be subservient to expression; on the subject of *Poésie pour Pouvoir* he makes no secret of his dissatisfaction with the recorded tape, but at the same time speaks of his intention to consider electro-acoustical research afresh; and in the case of *Livre pour quatuor* he reveals the creative thinking which led him to a far-reaching transformation of the work from the moment when, for practical reasons of performance, he decided to transfer it to a string orchestra so that it became *Livre pour cordes*.

He has already conducted his own auto-critique elsewhere, but this was in order to justify changes of direction in his activities as a composer. What one understands better now is Boulez's determination to keep an open mind towards all his works, his willingness to rewrite them so as to keep everything in line with the general scheme of his creative work and to obtain an overall coherence.

In reply to his interviewer's questions, Boulez the 'radical' composer is nevertheless led to place himself in a Western musical tradition, not so much in relation to his immediate predecessors as through a conception of artistic creation which links him with the large forms in German music, as in Bach, Beethoven or Berg: for him, as for them, composition is a burgeoning proliferation, an efflorescent yet controlled amplification, growing out of small initial cells. So one is less surprised to find that, contrary to what one had supposed, Boulez feels closer to Berg than to Webern and limits the influence of Debussy on his own music to certain inventive processes and refinements of orchestration. But on the whole, Boulez does not call into question either his past enthusiasms or his fundamental repulsions. He confirms his hostility to every kind of academicism, lumping together Stravinsky's neo-classicism and Schoenberg's tradition-bound formalism; but he no longer finds it necessary to launch into impassioned denunciations on the subject. For him, every reclamation of the past is hateful: he is therefore also opposed to retrospective amalgams accepted by some composers of his own generation who for a while had appeared to be working on the same lines as himself.

At the same time he is mistrustful of the 'underground' movement and of the attempt by certain other contemporary musicians to condemn artistic creation, an attitude which leads them to indulge in an anachronistic kind of theatrical polemics and in peripheral attitudes. When Deliège confronts him with an Adorno-like dialectic, Boulez does not hesitate to oppose it, affirming that contemporary society does not inexorably force the artist to choose between becoming a slave to commercial interests or fighting in the underground movement. (Does not the 'underground' in any case quickly contrive to establish its own commercial network?) In fact, as he himself says, Boulez is prepared to 'enter into the system' but only in order to 'try and change it from the inside'.

No doubt Boulez is here justifying all those undertakings which have linked him with more or less official 'institutions': his lively contribution to the artistic life of Paris through the 'Domaine musical' concerts, his compositions for German radio, his conducting appointments at the BBC and in New York, and his career as a touring conductor. Yet Boulez has good cause to make the point that by demanding a high level of professionalism in the performance of contemporary music he has helped to make it better known and has been able to seize the bastions that had been closed to it.

Boulez repeatedly insists on the importance of professionalism in musicians — notably in his remarks on musical education, which have not previously appeared, and where he contrasts in a happy phrase the 'deliberately' self-taught and the 'accidentally' self-taught. One of the merits of these broadcast interviews is that they show us a Boulez who is freer than in his critical writings (sometimes too concerned with short-term objectives), a Boulez closer to the man he is in daily life and in his conversations as an artist: perhaps less concerned with the intransigent defence of particular theses, but extremely coherent in his overall conceptions. Through these conversations comes a clear picture of Boulez's uncompromising fidelity towards what he has aspired to be since he first made his appearance in the world of music: a creative artist opposed to all forms of academicism and imposing the greatest degree of discipline on himself to achieve the greatest degree of freedom.

Robert Wangermée

CHAPTER I
THE FORMATIVE YEARS

Célestin Delìege: Pierre Boulez, as we are about to embark on a retrospect of your works, it may be a good idea to start from the beginning – perhaps about the time of the end of the war – in 1945.

Generally your biographers have recorded that at a given moment the young engineering student went over to the Conservatoire to study music. However, the reasons which led to this change of direction are not so well known. We know that from childhood you had been in contact with music a great deal, but does this explain everything?

Pierre Boulez: The change of direction is very simple to explain. It is something I had wanted for quite a long time, and I should make it clear that I only prepared for the Ecole polytechnique and did not actually go there. I am not a 'college man' as you might say; I was too young for that. I simply did the one year of preparation and at seventeen found myself free to choose my own destiny; free, at any rate, to choose music as the main function of my existence. So it was not a belated decision taken after much hesitation, but one already deeply rooted in me as a result solely of my early musical education – very ordinary as it happened, since it took place in a tiny provincial town, without any contact with what one might call day-to-day musical life. You can imagine that in France, before the 1939 war, the musical activity in a town of seven thousand inhabitants was extremely small: there were practically no concerts. All one could do was learn the piano; in my case I did this while attending secondary school. After a time this brought me into contact with some amateur musicians – as we call them, and it is a splendid name [because in French *amateurs de musique* also carries the con--notation 'music-lovers' – Translator] – and I played chamber music with them. In this way I broadened my horizons a little: instead of knowing only the piano repertory I became familiar with the field of chamber music fairly early. At the same time, since I went to a Catholic school, there was a choir in which I sang and this brought me into contact with vocal music – not always very good vocal music, but even so a certain amount of it was worthwhile.

These different levels of musical involvement probably instilled in me, while I was still very young – at an age when one hardly imagines becoming a professional musician and does not think in those terms at all – the idea of making music the centre of my existence and not just an episodic activity. So the decision goes back a long way, almost to my childhood, and this being so I really had no hesitation. After a certain age when, after all, the authority of the family counts for less, you know perfectly well that you must decide on your own existence.

CD: You referred in passing to the religious establishment where you received your schooling. I think it would not be disclosing any secret to say that a Catholic education could hardly have been in keeping with your philosophical convictions, nor with your development. We know that you feel a spiritual affinity with Joyce. In this establishment, did you have an experience which was – even remotely – similar of that of Stephen Daedalus?

PB: The catalysing experience described in *Portrait of the Artist as a Young Man* is one common to many young people who have been educated in relatively strict religious establishments and have failed to benefit greatly from it – in the first place because little in it coincided with their personal convictions, and secondly because it involved a frame of action and of reference which already seemed to them quite out of date. Of course matters were much less acute than they are today: there was neither rebellion nor collective disapproval of the sort that we have seen since. Some more independent characters were fairly quick to reject every kind of formal observance. What struck me most was that it was so mechanical: there was a total absence of genuine conviction behind it. It was a parody, and when you are young you feel this far more acutely because you want a way of life bearing some relation to your beliefs. Later one learns to adapt oneself somehow or other. One way in which education can mark you – at any rate, it did me – is precisely its inability to combine an existence of real meaning with observances

11

which have lost all their ethical content.

CD: And yet at the time you refrained from polemics against the system?

PB: When you are thirteen or fourteen and feeling a bit isolated, your first thought is to make the most you can of the educational conditions in order to lead your own personal life. In those days, in any case, one did not think of connecting one's difficulties with the system, with the validity of the system itself. One's first re-action at that age was to try to escape from a framework that was clearly uncongenial, but without going so far as to call into question the framework itself.

CD: My reason for asking about this was to find out whether there were, when you were adolescent, any early signs of the polemical attitude which you have constantly shown throughout your career. But since we are here to discuss your music, let us now return to that.

I note that in discussing the starting point of your music your biographers speak mostly — and with good reason — of the in-fluence of Messiaen and Webern. These are indeed the influences you yourself acknowledged at the time. Nevertheless what is immediately obvious, even on a fairly perfunctory examination of the works, is that, although you do take up Messiaen's increased range of rhythmic possibilities, you by no means impose his rhythmic disciplines; and although the influence of Webern is there, and is preponderant, the scores show no sign of the Webern-ian 'void' — on the contrary, your scores are exceedingly densely written and you did not hesitate to adopt large-scale forms.

PB: I think that these are influences one undergoes and at the same time rejects. If one is gifted with a sort of creative instinct (basically a thing that cannot be precisely explained) this kind of reaction is natural: it means that you assimilate what attracts you and what is necessary, while rejecting constraints that don't seem fruitful enough. This would describe my attitude to Messiaen and Webern at that time. But there is more to it than that: when you first encounter such works — Messiaen's just as much as Webern's — you don't quite grasp their scope, nor probably their logic. There is a difference of age. For instance, looking at music composed by

Webern when he was about fifty, it is very difficult for a nineteen-
or twenty-year-old to assimilate it as a total object. When you are
young you are like a bird of prey, seizing on what suits you and
leaving aside what doesn't.

As for Messiaen's system, it must be remembered that it had not
yet been worked out as completely as it was a few years later –
from 1948 or 1949, even 1950. I was in his class in 1944 and made
enormous use of the quite exceptional rhythmic elaboration
already present in his scores, but there was not yet the rigorous
control that he was to put into certain later constructions.

CD: Even so, there were already what I call constraints: for instance, the non-retrogradable rhythms, the thesaurus of Indian
rhythm, and so forth. At any rate, you did not keep to these types
of structure in any literal way . . .

PB: As a matter of fact, that side of Messiaen has never much
interested me. As you know, he very often makes use of rhythms
drawn from either Greek or Indian music, and to my way of
thinking this poses a problem. It is very difficult to introduce
fragments of another civilisation into a work. This is what I
believe now, but I also believed it then: we have to invent our own
rhythmic vocabulary in accordance with our own norms. In this
sense, even in my earliest works, there is what one might call a
contrast between free forms (sometimes there are, for instance,
extremely free rhythms – almost improvised, or written down
as they are thought up) and on the other hand extremely strict
sections. This is something I still practise; it is one of my main
ideas. Even in my first published composition, the Sonatina for
flute and piano, there are certain passages made up of elaborate,
highly-developed rhythmic structures; these are still worked out
in a simple way, being based on straightforward schemes and
written in a classical style, but even so they are elaborated to the
limit of their potential. A little later I had further ideas on the
subject, but from then on I already considered that rhythmic
writing ought to be something worked on for its own sake, and I
think this is the lesson I learnt from Messiaen, particularly from
his classes on music from Stravinsky onwards. After having analysed *The Rite of Spring* with him, or even his own works, I was
convinced of the necessity of working at purely rhythmic in-

13

vention.

Moreover, in the Webern pieces I knew at that time, I had not found that type of very dense rhythmic structure — though it does exist in works by Webern that I discovered later. (It must be remembered that at that time Webern was still an unknown composer, and his scores were very difficult to come by.) In the first works I got to know — the Symphony op. 21 for example — the rhythmic writing is extremely classical: it consists of canons such as can be found above all in pre-classical or Baroque music. In fact there is not really any very profound rhythmic elaboration in the whole of the modern Viennese school.

But another thing that attracted me was what Berg called 'monorythmica' — used in certain passages of his music, and above all in *Wozzeck* — in which a whole train of musical thought is angled towards a single rhythmic sequence; here we have a proliferating object which can thus impart unity to musical ideas or even completely encompass them. I was very struck with Berg's discovery, but nothing else held my attention until I discovered the last works of Webern, and in particular the Variations op. 30, where there is a very close rhythmic weave and a truly exciting way of writing.

From my contact with Messiaen, then, I had taken only what could be of service to me — namely, his work on rhythmic cells and their modification, interpolation, partial augmentation, diminution, and so on. From Webern, on the other hand, I had taken a particular conception, not of silence (in which I was not specially interested — it seemed to me that silence, in Webern, was something peculiarly his own which would be difficult to use without becoming imitative) but of a certain texture of intervals. Beyond this, the dynamic character of my early works is really quite different from the agogics found in Webern. I had no inclination for vague objects or states of mind, but preferred extremely dynamic works whose texture would therefore be sufficiently dense to propel this dynamism further and further forward.

CHAPTER II
PREFERENCES AND JUDGMENTS

CD: This inclination towards extremely dynamic forms is perhaps what has led you to produce such intensively worked-out scores?

PB: Yes, I have what is probably an innate feeling for what one might call the proliferation of basic materials. This means that in general I start off with relatively simple materials; my basic ideas, and even the overall plan of my works, are fairly simple, but of course within the plan there will be very highly developed textures. When I have in front of me a musical idea or a kind of musical expression to be given to a particular text of my own invention, I discover in the text, when submitting it to my own kind of analysis and looking at it from every possible angle, more and more possible ways of varying it, transforming it, augmenting it and making it proliferate. For me a musical idea is like a seed which you plant in compost, and suddenly it begins to proliferate like a weed. Then you have to thin it out. I find it difficult to keep to very cut-and-dried developments, by which I mean to see composition from a negative rather than a positive standpoint. I realise that a tendency towards proliferation has its dangers because it can lead one always towards the same type of density, in other words a density that is extreme at every moment, an extreme of tension or of variation. So in many cases I have found it necessary to reduce, to thin out the possibilities, or else to put one after the other so as to create an evolution in time and not a superposition that would have been too compact.

CD: Would you not say that the true precedent for such proliferation in European music was Johann Sebastian Bach?

PB: I think that the works of J. S. Bach are the greatest model — in particular the way in which he manages to create an entire form from very little, from very few ideas. The pieces that made a great impression on me, and perhaps still impress me most in his entire output, are the chorale variations and chorale preludes. In a fugue, the construction is stricter in that it starts out

15

from a defined plan; not, of course, that all the fugues are built on the same model (it has been pointed out often enough that each fugue is slightly different from the next), but even so the form is always pre-established. In the chorale there is likewise the phrase to be developed; and what is remarkable in Bach is that the further he progresses the deeper he gets into the meaning of his text so as to bring out its full potential. Thus we meet with extended textures that are practically continuous throughout their length – these are absolutely extraordinary: take the 'Catechism' Preludes from the *Clavierübung*, for instance: they are truly prodigious from this point of view. These, for me, are the crowning achievement. In this respect I would place them above the *Art of Fugue* and the *Musical Offering*.

CD: Higher even than the *Mass in B minor*?

PB: Yes, certainly.

CD: Yet it contains the proliferation you speak of, and to a very high degree.

PB: Yes; but it is moulded, so to speak, into stricter and more clear-cut forms. For instance, the Kyrie is a fugue on a very broad scale, and what follows is not a large-scale form such as Beethoven tried to create by fitting together all the sections of the Mass but each section is a kind of cell worked out on its own account. In other words, one verse of the Credo will correspond to one musical form, another to a different form, and so on, so that as yet there is no attempt as was to come later with Beethoven and above all Wagner towards a vast continuity in time with all the sections of a work merging into each other; in proceeding from one verse to another there is a kind of dissolution and a very abrupt contrast. In the chorale preludes, on the other hand, there is a real continuity over a fairly large time-span and I find this deeply impressive. It is due specifically to the development of the chorale phrases and to nothing else; it is not based on a preconceived form.

CD: This is very interesting, because your biographers have tended rather to look for influence on your music in that of your immediate predecessors. Of course, here it goes beyond the question of influences, to the fact that you belong to a particular musical civilisation.

PB: I would say personally — and this is perhaps strange, since people always say that you are very much influenced by your national culture — that I feel that, when it comes to form, German music has influenced me by far the most — and the most German features of German music at that!

CD: It is probably in this music that one finds the most solid types of form.

PB: The most solid and the best established — at any rate, the most remarkable from the point of view of continuity. In general the French contribution to music is a kind of form that is relatively clear, compact and easy to establish. Personally, however, my preference would go much more to forms capable of transformation that you find, for instance, used by Berg in such a striking manner. I have undergone a sort of evolution in reverse. At first I was very much attracted to the vocabulary of Webern; I found him extremely important at that time, particularly because he laid the foundations of an indispensable musical grammar and vocabulary. But I always found that the more Webern went on the simpler his forms became — too simple for my liking. For example, in Webern there are forms consisting of a first section, a central section and then a third section which is simply a variation of the first; or else there will be a series of variations. Now even if the variations are extremely subtle and contain cross-references between themselves they still remain what I call 'compartmentalised' forms, in other words forms which, although there may be development from one to the next, are still divided off and clearly established for a certain space of time. On the other hand what I find in Berg, for example, is a sense of continuous development with an enormous degree of ambiguity — what I call a 'romanesque' or novel-like development — that is, we no longer have a simple architectural development with points of symmetry (always an easy standpoint to adopt) but on the contrary we have much more intricate forms which virtually never cease to develop and imply no return to earlier material. That is the great discovery of the German tradition. It is just this 'point of no return' in music which progressively became the problem for Beethoven and then the central problem for Wagner. All Berg did was to make this

17

problem of continuity even more explicit by combining forms that were very much established and, as a rule, clear and preconceived, with an acute sense of development. And this produces an ambiguity that is exceptionally interesting, especially in an opera like *Wozzeck*, but also in the Chamber Concerto or the *Lyric Suite* — his three greatest works, I think, as far as form is concerned: all three are extraordinary because they show a sense of development rarely to be found in music, and this side of Berg attracted me a great deal. That is why — in a quite different direction — I am attracted, too, by Debussy's *Jeux*: because it was the first time, I think, that he kept for such a long stretch to a completely continuous form, and this is what I believe to be important.

FORM

CD: If it were not for Rameau and Debussy, would it be possible to speak of form in French music at all?

PB: In French music it is naturally assumed that Rameau represents a form. Yet compared with Bach's, Rameau's form is not at all satisfactory since it is terribly limited in its perception and in its articulation. The excessive use of dance music in Rameau's operas makes for such very marked and predictable sections that in the end one very quickly loses interest. On the other hand, what *is* interesting about Rameau in this context is the great suppleness of his recitatives. They are well worth studying to see how he managed to escape from this constructional problem, which elsewhere he dealt with so awkwardly, and to understand how he achieved dramatic truth in continuity.

As for Debussy's forms, these too are usually fairly clear. He never really explored very far in that direction.

There is another composer who is much less talked about — Berlioz. I must say that for a Frenchman he could not be further from what is known as the 'French tradition'. On the whole, Berlioz's forms are utterly preposterous in comparison with what might be termed a certain classicism, a certain obviousness of form. Of course I mean early Berlioz — not the Berlioz of *Les Troyens*, who is very disappointing in this respect, but the Berlioz of the *Symphonie Fantastique* and of *Harold en Italie*. At times even the Berlioz of *La Damnation de Faust* is quite invaluable because he clearly proves that in fact there is no 'French tradition' — absolutely none.

18

One can find a certain continuity in the way the German tradition understands music, but it would be very difficult to see any continuity in the way the French have seen it. In France each individual has understood music in his own way, but there has been no continuity of perception — probably because the different stages have been widely separated. If you look at the dates: there is Rameau, then a long time afterwards Berlioz, and a long time after that Debussy; obviously that does not make for continuity. By contrast the German tradition has real continuity. To talk of continuity in the French tradition you have to go back to the sixteenth century. By the seventeenth century it had practically ended. In the sixteenth century, however — one might even say between the thirteenth and seventeenth centuries — there was a continuity in the tradition of writing; after that, I personally find none. To my way of thinking, I repeat, it is quite mad to speak of a 'French tradition'.

If we are thinking in terms of characteristics rather than of tradition, then one of the constant features of French musical expression since the eighteenth century — whenever it has been in competent hands — has been a preoccupation with sound itself. Berlioz's earliest instrumental writing, for instance, is extraordinarily imaginative compared with everything that was going on around him; even if his technique of composition is clumsy, or his harmony sometimes dreadful, his inventiveness in handling the physiology of the orchestra is far beyond anything achieved by his predecessors. If one looks closely at Berlioz's sources — of which he speaks so often (he talks a lot about Beethoven and about Weber, and also speaks of Gluck) — to find all the examples he quotes of the use of instruments that have influenced him (the use of the clarinet in Weber, a certain way of using the strings in Beethoven and so on), one can see the astonishing power of imagination with which he added his own vision right from the start. From the *Symphonie Fantastique* on, Berlioz took the instrumentation of his day in hand and pushed it forward to an extraordinarily new level. If we compare Berlioz's orchestra with that of his near-contemporary Schumann — I have chosen this example quite deliberately — they are as different as chalk from cheese. In the one case there is a prodigious instrumental imagination, and in the other something colourless. Of course Schumann's

19

orchestration is adequate for what he wants to do, but you feel clearly that his thinking never went very far in that direction.

On the other hand, as I have said, there are awkward harmonies in Berlioz that make one scream; it is easy to see that he picked out his chords on the guitar and could hear almost nothing. It is all very well to claim that Berlioz's unusual chordal placing is a sign of his 'genius': I think rather that it was clumsiness. He invents melodies that contain certain references to Weber or to Beethoven, then harmonises them in an extremely clumsy way; so in his case, melodic and harmonic invention do not coincide. We do not find, as in Schumann, the invention of a melody which carries its own harmony; that does not exist in Berlioz, and this demonstrates that some temperaments have a gift for invention in one sphere and not in another. This emerges very clearly from these two particular cases.

Debussy's orchestration, on the other hand, when compared with even such brilliant contemporaries as Strauss and Mahler (who knew all about orchestration) shows an infinitely fresher imagination: his sense of instrumentation is less ordinary. Although Strauss's instrumentation is extraordinarily brilliant and Mahler's highly ingenious, neither possesses the novelty you find even in Debussy's less complex orchestral works such as the *Prélude à l'après-midi d'un faune* or the *Nocturnes,* which presents a sonority and a relationship between the instruments that were quite unknown before him; whereas, for all Mahler's ingeniousness and Strauss's brilliance, their world is full of references to Romanticism: their instrumentation derives directly from Wagner or Brahms. Debussy's instrumentation, although it too is sometimes derivative, particularly from *Parsifal,* is conceived from quite a different point of view: the number of instruments, their balance, the order in which they are used, their use itself, produces a *different climate*. There is also, particularly in Debussy's case, the fact that he invents directly in orchestral terms – as can be clearly seen in the evolution between his sketches, which are like reduced short scores, and his finished scores. For instance I have compared the sketches for *La Mer* with the finished score, and it is quite plain that there are a whole host of small figurations and motifs that were added to the instrumentation at the last minute. This is not just a matter of preparing an orchestral version from a score that is already completely defined, as happens with Ravel; the difference is that in Debussy's case the sketches, though complete from the compositional point of view, still need the illumination of the orchestra before the work acquires its real dimensions and true relief. This is a procedure peculiar to both Berlioz and Debussy. One also finds in Berlioz certain instrumental ideas that are an integral part of the composition rather than a surface veneer. I think there is an important difference between the two attitudes: when instrumentation has become such an integral part of composition that the work acquires from the instrumentation not a kind of acoustical enrichment but a formal and functional one, then one can say that real progress has been made.

CD: Hearing you speak of the great forms of German music a few moments ago, I thought of an objection Adorno would raise. If he were still there to hear you, he would not fail to point out that this concern of yours to refer constantly to the logical, rational element in major musical forms is also a way of preserving a certain *status quo*, that may show conservative intentions. To what extent would this objection of a post-Hegelian philosopher be valid?

PB: To try to preserve these forms at all costs would naturally be a conservative attitude because they would be meaningless compared with what they had been capable of expressing at an earlier period. What is interesting in Berg, for example, is not that he preserved these forms, but that he charged them with so much ambiguity that they take on a totally different meaning and virtually cease to exist. This evolution accomplished by Berg can only be seen as part of a continual quest for maximum effectiveness in these forms, which is no sooner found than there is only one desire – to progressively break up and destroy them, or to so overload them with emotional and formal additions that they collapse under all the extra weight. History as it is made by great composers is not a history of conservation but of destruction – even while cherishing what is destroyed. I would compare this phenomenon of historical evolution with objects put in a chalky spring. If the object is fairly simple, ordinary even, such as a stone or an egg, it will suddenly acquire a new form. The first stage of petrification will transform it into something marvellous and beautifully

21

balanced: this unpretentious object will assume a 'perfect' form. But then, the spring continues to run and the object gradually becomes a monstrosity as it is encrusted with limestone; it becomes what we would call 'baroque' — in other words, its function no longer justifies this proliferation. It becomes overloaded with emotiveness and the desire to gradually change its function, and at a certain moment it becomes so saturated that it has no further meaning; then one moves away to find something else. This is how it has been with all forms of expression. In architecture, for instance, evolution is always based on certain simple principles, which become ever more overloaded until they finally collapse and give birth to something simple again. The difference between baroque and classical art is this need to conserve a certain type of design long enough for it to prove its uselessness. To my way of thinking, historical continuity is based precisely on this excess of tension which collapses abruptly, begins again from zero, and recharges itself until the next point of collapse. For me, history is not at all a continuing process, but rather a wave-form that passes through positive points, falls back to zero, then moves through negative points and then back again, etc... My vision of history is in fact sine-shaped, or else helical — I am not sure what you would call it . . . .

CD: I think your answer would have satisfied Adorno, since this goes to the root of the dialectical principle. Contradiction, after all, is fertile.

PB: That's right.

CHAPTER III
IN DEFENCE OF BERG

CD: All through this conversation you have spoken a great deal about Berg. Now we are going to talk about a stage in your development at which you were hardly prepared to recognise the value of Berg. There was the article you wrote in the second number of the magazine *Polyphonie*[1] — an article which made a great impact at the time — in which Berg received harsh treatment at the hands of the polemicist you already were. However, you now seem to have modified your position. Is this because your work as a conductor has led you to see Berg in a different way, or have you perhaps kept to your original position only as regards certain aspects of Berg's work?

PB: No; I returned to Berg before I started conducting him, in fact when I analysed *Wozzeck* for my pupils in Basle in 1960. *Wozzeck* is in any case a work that has always fascinated me (in good ways as well as bad). But above all (and especially in 1945) I was very deeply irritated by its Romanticism, and particularly for quite external reasons to do with social climate. In that difficult period when people denied the value of Schoenberg, and of Webern even more, only Berg of the Viennese school found justification in their eyes because, it was said, he was 'human', he was 'the only one who wrote music', he was concerned with 'expression' and so forth. (You have heard these arguments as often as I have, and they were extremely irritating.) That was one of the reasons why I went into battle. This indulgence — a romanticism which you can put between as many inverted commas as you like — was the delight of the musical world and caused it to wallow in Berg but not Webern. It was this that drove me to write what I did. Moreover I was perfectly aware that to discover a new vocabulary it was no use looking to Berg, since from that point of view he represented the end of a world, if I may put it that way.

It was only later — I have already mentioned how one takes from people what one wants — that I was attracted to Berg's complexity. I well remember how, very early on, in 1948 — very shortly after the article you have quoted — I made a study of the Chamber Concerto; this was the first time I had had access to the score for any length of time, and the work gave me a great deal to think about; I found that there was a lot more to Berg than his immediately accessible romanticism. As I continued to make more discoveries, what thrilled me as I went along was the complexity of his mind: the number of internal correspondences, the intricacy of his musical construction, the esoteric character of many of his references, the density of texture, that whole universe in per-petual motion revolving constantly around itself, all this is abso-lutely fascinating. It is a universe that is never completed, always in expansion — a world so profound, dense and rich and inex-haustible that one can, after thorough analysis, still come back to it a third or fourth time to find fleeting references that one had not noticed before.

Webern's work, on the other hand, once one has grasped its essence and its vocabulary (and of course I am referring par-ticularly to the last works), does not require a series of different readings. It is like a picture by Mondrian. You can see its per-fection and it is very striking, being stripped down to the absolute minimum — a truly austere kind of perfection; but when you see it again at a later date, it offers you nothing further. At least that is my view: that is what I get out of it. The next time I see the picture it is the same — there aren't any different levels of inter-pretation.

On the other hand (and I am deliberately taking an example from a period which no longer concerns me) if I look at certain paintings by Cézanne, their complexity, their references, their infinity of architectural and textural detail all offer so many levels of interpretation that I can look at them five times, ten times, and still feel that I have not accounted for every small detail of their texture. Well, there are often times in Berg when I have this impression of an extremely difficult work, whose texture is very hard to grasp completely. Despite the fact that they communicate so readily to the listener, Berg's are works to go back to five or six times, especially the large-scale ones.

This idea of 'levels of interpretation' is a very important one for me. I have said often enough that I like a work to be a labyrinth — one should be able to lose oneself in it. A work whose course reveals itself completely at one hearing is flat and lacking in mystery. The mystery of a work resides precisely in its being valid at many different levels. Whether it be a book, a picture or a piece of music, these polyvalent levels of interpretation are fundamental to my conception of the work.

CD: It might be said, then, that if the musical world cultivated Berg at that time, seeing him as the only 'human' composer of the three Viennese, it was because they did not perceive the deeper levels of his work. However, your fight at that time went beyond opposition to an accepted point of view; for example, I remember that you attacked the passage in the Violin Concerto where there is a contradiction of language between the Bach chorale[2] and the violin part set against it. Do you now find greater virtue in this kind of co-existence between different grammars and styles within this work?

PB: No. I am still firmly convinced that such co-existence is impossible. In the case you mention it is a *dramatic gesture*. I do not think it a very profound gesture — indeed I find rather that it expresses anxiety; perhaps even rejection of the norms of contemporary behaviour. There is a sort of nostalgia for a bygone world that you find again much later in works of quite recent date. A friend of mine had a very good expression for it: 'there are some composers who feel they simply must revive the *gruppetto*'. I find this a pretty caustic way of putting it, but extremely apt, since attempts to recuperate the past have absolutely no interest for the future. To my way of thinking, if one is to preserve certain aspects of the past and to integrate them into our present-day thought, it must be done in the most abstract terms. For instance, one might take a scheme combining strict writing — perhaps canonic — with free writing as being an interesting form from the past. It is quite valid to want to retain the principle of canonic writing, and it will entail a very strict responsibility towards the intervals one writes. This kind of 'rediscovery' I would accept but, for all that, I am not going to write academic canons. Likewise it is possible to rediscover harmonic functions.

This was indeed rather a weak point with the three Viennese — they had other preoccupations, of course. Take the melodic themes in Schoenberg — for instance the theme of the Orchestral

Variations op. 31: this is a melody, and Schoenberg thought it sufficient to add the chromatically complementary notes in order to provide a suitable harmony. It was a kind of dogma in the abstract by which he would write three or six notes, and then add the other six, and call the result functional harmony. But harmonic functions have quite a different nature and are not merely functions of complementarity. If we want to rediscover harmonic functions – and it is in fact of very great importance that we should – we must realise that they cannot be found in our existing vocabulary by simply trying to reintroduce the cycle of fifths or by returning to the vocabulary of expanded tonality and making it say what it cannot express. Such means lead to a complete contradiction: they give rise to connotations which not only destroy the unity of style but also break up the aesthetic project in hand. In this sense there will be centrifugal forces in the composition that there is no way of unifying. Occasionally, perhaps – but by no means always – painters have been able to attempt collages with sufficiently neutral materials. Usually in such cases they have taken a material that could be integrated into a fresh form precisely by virtue of its neutrality. But by definition, musical material is not neutral. It expresses a quality of style, and as soon as that quality is inserted into a more general type of material then there is a gap: in other words this patched-on bit of music will simply disintegrate and then not only will it lack any overall function that might appear as some particular reference to some particular style, but the music will be pulverised into bits and pieces devoid of all formal unity – because even form in music is essentially dependent upon the material. When that material is a series of bits and pieces, the form too becomes a patchwork.

So in fact my point of view has not altered at all since the time you speak of; on the contrary, I am perhaps even more severe now than I was then: I am less and less interested in nostalgia!

26

CHAPTER IV
THE RELEVANCE OF SCHOENBERG

CD: I would like to consider your first creative period for a moment longer, to look at your Sonatina for flute and piano. You have already spoken of the rhythmic procedures fathered, if I may put it that way, by Messiaen; but you have also acknowledged that you took Schoenberg's First Chamber Symphony as your model for this work. I suppose this must have been a formal model chosen for objective reasons?

PB: Yes, entirely. When I wrote the Sonatina I wanted to compose a continuous piece, and I had been much impressed by Schoenberg's Chamber Symphony precisely because it shows the ambiguity that can be achieved within a single form. In this work you have the four movements of a sonata, but at the same time these four movements constitute the four stanzas, the four developments of a single movement. Thus he creates an ambiguity between a small form and a large one. That is what attracted me. Naturally I had no desire to copy Schoenberg's plan, but rather to pass through the same experience myself and see how far you would have to push this ambiguity of form for it to become something new. In the Sonatina I did this just with the initial basic material – which was very simple as it happens. What I particularly wanted to find out was how such material could be expanded in one direction or another, in other words to give it a kind of elasticity that would make it suitable for a variety of tasks. Really there is just one basic idea which becomes a first theme, a sort of sonata allegro, then a second which becomes a scherzo; this same material is transformed in turn into a scherzo, a slow movement and a finale. What interested me were the transformations of a single theme, and from that point of view the work is even more unified than the Chamber Symphony because there is less basic material. Yes, it is quite true that Schoenberg's Chamber Symphony was a great influence on me at the time from a formal standpoint.

But unless you know the influence to be Schoenberg's, I don't think anyone would be able to guess it at first sight: you just

27

notice the four forms, nothing more. For the rest, any stylistic influence is absolutely non-existent. The Chamber Symphony is in a post-Romantic idiom, and this aspect of it did not influence me at all. I have always had a tendency to separate the formal context very clearly from the ideas themselves, although I know full well that in composition style is intimately bound up with form; I conduct a sort of chemical dissociation to help me to seize and retain what interests me and to drop what does not. Moreover my music repeatedly contains references to designs or ideas that are completely removed from their context. At that time the post-Romanticism of the Chamber Symphony did not interest me very much. Nowadays I would be more indulgent, because it is further away, and holds no temptations for me. What did attract me immensely, on the other hand, was Schoenberg's invention of a continuous form evolved from symphonic movements. That is what I found in this work, and that is what I took in order to do something on the same lines.

CD: The dissociation you speak of between form and language — to put it in even more schematic terms — was certainly confirmed at the time of the first performance of the Sonatina for flute and piano in Brussels in 1947. It was greeted, as I remember, with a great many reservations, if not booing, and in consequence the work was for a long time taboo to concert organisers in Brussels. Yet at that time the public already responded to Schoenberg's works with relative politeness or relative indifference — which is its usual attitude.

PB: Yes, but the difference was more a question of a state of mind — thank goodness, since the Chamber Symphony was composed in 1906 and this Sonatina in 1946. If nothing had happened in forty years of music it would have been pretty catastrophic. There is nothing unusual in the fact that a work written in 1946 should be very different from one written in 1906. What is unusual is that Schoenberg's work should have remained virtually unknown for so long for aesthetic reasons. That is why I took up Schoenberg's defence so ardently for a while and then dropped him when I had had enough of defending him. For quite some time it was said — especially among French circles in Paris — that this music had nothing to offer us since it was so much a part of the Central

European tradition that it was completely at odds with French culture. I personally cannot think of a sillier way of seeing things. Even if works are quite alien to your way of being and thinking, anyone concerned with his own personal development must confront these works, not only to discover his own truth and try to rid himself of the uneasiness he may feel when faced with certain things that appear unnatural to him, but also to grasp what permanent value they may hold. The truth is — and here I apologise for using slightly outmoded terms — that one must distinguish between the essence of things: what may have permanence, and what aspect of their existence is merely of the times. Thus for me the post-Romanticism one sometimes comes across — and notably in the Chamber Symphony — is a thing of the times, above all now! But the fact that Schoenberg invented such an elaborate and continuous symphonic form I still find extremely striking.

CD: Schoenberg also came to my mind when I was looking through your First Piano Sonata. I do not know what your conscious references were; I personally thought above all of pre-serial Schoenberg — the Schoenberg of the earlier piano pieces of the op. 23 set for instance. What brings these pieces to mind is the intervallic writing in your First Sonata.

PB: Yes, these were amongst the pieces I was particularly studying at the period. But previously I had discovered Schoenberg's op. 11. This was on my piano for a long time, and the Sonata shows its influences very clearly, even if it lacks the Romantic hypertension of the op. 11 pieces. It was the third of these pieces, and also of course the op. 23 pieces, which led me towards a pianistic style quite different from what I saw around me — with the exception, to be fair, of Messiaen's writing for the piano (not his musical vocabulary in general). Beyond that, my interest in Schoenberg dwindles a great deal. I do not find the Suite op. 25 particularly attractive. The op. 23 pieces, however, and above all the first four of them, are quite extraordinary. Even so, I still prefer the third piece of op. 11, which I regard as a great achievement. It puts one in mind of the piece that concludes the second part of *Pierrot Lunaire*, 'Die Kreuze', in which there is an immense piano solo. This is written in exactly the same manner — in a pianistic style that impressed me enormously when I read it. One feels the

29

affinity immediately — that is, a kind of piano writing unheard-of for the period, with considerable density of texture and a violence of expression because the piano is treated not as Stravinsky treated it, as a percussion instrument, but as a percussive piano which is at the same time remarkably prone to frenzy. I would say that it is the instrument of frenzy *par excellence*, both in the third piece of op. 11 and in 'Die Kreuze' from *Pierrot Lunaire*. I found Schoenberg's writing for the piano very exciting at that time; I need hardly tell you that I find it less exciting in, for example, works such as the Piano Concerto.

CD: As you have just mentioned, there was a period during which you accepted Schoenberg; and then came a fairly violent rejection, resulting in your article 'Schoenberg est mort'[3] of 1951. What is your present position with regard to that article and with regard to Schoenberg?

PB: It is exactly the same. In Schoenberg's music there is a period which I find very exciting, and that is the whole period stretching roughly from 1907-1908 up to 1920; the last work of his that is really of great interest to me — and for very ambiguous reasons — is the Serenade op. 24. After that I find Schoenberg very difficult to swallow because of his constant academicism and above all his timidity after making his discovery. I would now no longer indulge in polemics on the subject — the lava has cooled and there is no point in starting further volcanoes. There is a phenomenon in Schoenberg's life that is very apparent from the fact that his style became academic. Instead of going forward, he stuck to constant factors: those rhythms of quite insufferable squareness, the diminished level of invention, the style, and finally the contrapuntal procedures which are academic and appear on every page (not just one page in ten but virtually ten in ten). One thing struck me very quickly: if you compare, for instance, the *Three Satires* op. 28 with the Four Pieces op. 27, written almost at the same time, you really wonder which is satire and which is serious; if you were to put the words of op. 27 to the music of op. 28 I don't think many people could sense the difference. I would even say that, personally, I don't much like even such extremely well-constructed and highly elaborate works as the Orchestral Variations op. 31, although I feel obliged to play it as I feel that people ought to be aware of and interested in a work of such concentration; but this is what I call an exercise in reclamation. I think I wrote as early as 1949[4] — which *is* fairly early after all — that Stravinsky's and Schoenberg's paths to neo-classicism differ basically only in one being diatonic and the other chromatic: for all practical purposes their itinerary is precisely the same.

Recently, after Stravinsky's death, I wrote an article[5] in which I compared Schoenberg's and Stravinsky's respective evolutions towards neo-classicism in very much more detail than I had done in 1949. I said that Stravinsky went about it like a dilettante going into a museum to look for material which he then took apart and reassembled in a different way. It was not a feeling for tradition that might have led him to reclaim this heritage. It was above all the need for what I call 'play'; he wanted to play with history because for the first time the riches of the past were all available. Schoenberg, on the other hand, tried to reinstate tradition. Thus his is a fundamentally different attitude, although the result is the same: both composers adopt dead forms, and because they are so obsessed with them they allow them to transform their musical ideas until these too are dead. Their musical invention has been virtually reshaped by old forms to the point where it suffers and dries up.

CD: Do you not think that this phenomenon of reclamation is typical of this century?

PB: There have been some attempts in the past but they were more ephemeral because the times were not ready for them. For instance, when Mozart discovered Bach or Handel he wrote an Overture in the style of Handel, which is really an early neo-classical overture[6].

CD: Yes, but the styles were compatible.

PB: Just so. And therefore the problem did not present itself in the same way. In Beethoven too we find a desire for archaism when he uses the Lydian mode, for example. But this deliberate archaism was based on very vague ideas, since he did not possess the documents on mediaeval music that we now have. He must certainly have read a treatise on the subject, but there is no reference to any particular work. Even so, from his point of view, there was a desire to go back to past history.

The two most striking examples in the nineteenth century – to which I refer in the article in question – are Berlioz's *L'Enfance du Christ* and Wagner's *The Mastersingers*. Berlioz even went so far as to give the first performance of his work under the name of an eighteenth-century *maître de chapelle*. However, it is very difficult to find traces of baroque style in *L'Enfance du Christ*; even so, this is deliberate archaism. It was the beginning of what came to be called 'suites in the ancient style'. There are a lot of them, and there can be no doubt that Stravinsky's neo-classicism, as well as Schoenberg's, is simply the end-result of the nineteenth century's discovery of the museum.

In the same way the Romantics rediscovered the Gothic style. At the end of the nineteenth century there were Gothic churches in profusion. This was the most striking example of stylistic reference. On the other hand, although in *The Mastersingers* there are no end of references to the *Minnesänger* and to the forms of sixteenth and – even more so – fifteenth century music, Wagner's music actually has nothing to do with the historical truth about the town of Nüremberg. This is why I feel really ill at ease when people try to depict the historical town on the stage when it is absent from the music. Clearly Wagner at one point felt an urge towards archaism, but the stylistic references were almost non-existent and never in danger of becoming heavy-handed.

Later, especially at the end of the nineteenth century and the beginning of the twentieth, an entire repertory that had previously been practically unexplored and unplayed was actually redis-covered: music began to cultivate a memory of its own. This feeling for the preservation of history that had already existed in literature for some time and had begun to happen in architecture also became a force in music. As a result, historical preservation brought with it the desire to reclaim the past in the present; and in the obvious form which it took it was the worst possible thing to do.

CD: Is this not also part of the conservative attitude peculiar to our own period (perhaps the most conservative of all time) in which people take up history in a literal manner rather than observing its profound currents?

PB: I believe that a civilisation which tends towards conservatism is a declining civilisation because it is afraid to go forward and ascribes more importance to its memories than to its future. Strong, expanding civilisations have no memory: they reject, they forget the past. They feel strong enough to be destructive because they know they can replace what has been destroyed. From this viewpoint our musical civilisation shows very distinct signs of decay since at all levels its emphasis on reclamation, even when wrapped in very general and broad considerations, shows that it has too many memories. I once pointed out, in a German magazine[7], that our Western civilisation would need Red Guards to get rid of a good number of statues or even decapitate them. The French Revolution decapitated statues in churches; one may regret this now, but it was proof of a civilisation on the march. When people will even collect the least knickerbocker-button from the eighteenth century that is something I personally find profoundly distasteful.

CD: But in fact, if we are faced with a phenomenon of civilisation, perhaps we should no longer reproach composers who attempt such reclamations with lack of awareness or even, more strongly, with irresponsibility – a term you have used, though perhaps not in reference to the same composers. Do they not simply arrive at a dead-end to which historical inevitability has led them?

PB: There is no such thing as historical inevitability. History is what one makes it. I hold very firmly to this principle. When someone speaks of being compelled by historical necessity it means he is no longer capable of acting for himself; in one sense history is something we enact, not something to be submitted to.

CD: Then a civilisation must prove itself by producing a sufficient number of individuals who display enough energy to maintain and prolong it. Do you think this is the present situation?

PB: In certain cases, yes; there still are people who have invention and are not over-concerned with the past. Naturally at a time like ours with mass communications – and here we touch on another problem – there are also a lot of people who are more concerned with conservation than with invention. It was not the same in

33

previous centuries, because communications were much more limited and art was not the central preoccupation of society that it has now become.

CHAPTER V
DIGRESSIONS ON MUSICAL EDUCATION

CD: We seem to be adopting the system of proliferation even in this conversation, so let us come back to our 'earlier cells'.

You have spoken of composers who were gifted with the instinct to create from the very start. Here you seem to have been something of a unique case. Unlike most composers you were not compelled — unless you have hidden them very thoroughly — to fill your drawers with scores that you no longer felt able to acknowledge — works that are usually called juvenilia and come before opus 1.

PB: There are some, but not many, because my musical development happened at the right time: I finished my studies while still young. I always tell my pupils that whatever one does in the way of studies — but especially in music — should be done quickly. There are very few things you can learn from a teacher. Personally I learnt all I could from a teacher in two years. After that I educated myself, naturally, but at twenty-one I had finished. This period (between the ages of eighteen and twenty-one) corresponded exactly with my discovery of the Viennese school, of Messiaen, of Stravinsky, and so on . . . in other words a whole repertory of whose existence I had been hardly aware at the age of seventeen. This discovery was very rapid, and that was my good luck. In two years my conceptions developed so much that what I composed in 1945 and 1946 I now consider as definitive for that period. I had no problems in this respect because, possibly by instinct, I had no hesitation over the choice to make. Sometimes such a choice can be worrying, but my critical powers were fairly alert. I made my choices instinctively and rationalised them afterwards. Twenty-five or twenty-seven years later, my preferences at that time as regards the music I knew remain virtually unchanged, though sometimes the emphasis has shifted. For example, Bartók played a role in my development that he can no longer have now: here the emphasis has shifted. But the five or six composers who influenced me the most are still those I personally find extremely

35

important.

CD: You seem to think of this period, which takes us back something like thirty years, as a happy one. Most of your colleagues, however, felt it to be a period of crisis. Moreover, you were virtually the only composer of your generation; the others began working from six to eight years later.

PB: Yes, I don't know why. In 1945 and 1946 my preferences were really quite precise, but since then certain differences have come about in the importance of things, in their hierarchical order, in what influences me more directly or less directly, and in things I now feel a greater affinity for than at that time; even so, my preferences were quite clear-cut, not only in music but also in literature and in painting.

The first time I saw paintings by Klee I was absolutely gripped by the force of his invention, and at that instant many other things fell to dust. It was in 1947, or perhaps slightly later, that I first saw paintings by Klee, Kandinsky and Mondrian; immediately I felt that here were three crucially important figures in the development of contemporary painting. For me they are still the most important painters of that period. Similarly my first encounters with Joyce, Kafka and – later – Musil made a real impression on me. I think I was fairly quick to define the world that preceded me, and this allowed me to make rapid progress because once the past has been got out of the way one need only think of oneself.

Once a certain level has been reached education has no further use, and this is what I later reiterated to my pupils during my three years at Basle. For all practical purposes you can learn all there is to be learnt from someone in the space of six months, and even that would be slow: sometimes a week is enough. After that, what counts most in the long run is hard work and personal preferences. When you have learnt certain skills of your craft you have to build on them and this education can only be done by yourself. I like people who are *deliberately self-taught* – that is, those who have the strength of will to have done with models that existed before them. But people who are *accidentally self-taught*, who have no knowledge of things, are of no interest to me at all, because they will never be rid of their predecessors. I might make a comparison with Genet's play *The Screens*. At a given moment the dead are represented as breaking through paper screens. I believe that to find one's true personality one has to break through the screens of preceding composers. Until this has been done one cannot be oneself: one has truly to die in this way, to break through the screens, in order to be reborn. Anyone who has not been through this experience, and has not done so early on, has missed something in my opinion.

CD: However, I must point out – and it is important to do so – that in Europe education is organised on the principle of complicated grading so that those who have to go through it are subjected to an exceedingly long-drawn-out process of education which, according to you, must hinder their development. Now for social reasons – sometimes perhaps simply because they do not belong to a privileged class, or for some other reason – they cannot refuse to go through this system. Do you not think that a great deal of potential is destroyed by the way education is organised?

PB: Yes – the whole system ought to be rethought. I am not familiar enough with the teaching of other subjects to say anything about this, but in music education is quite clearly organised in accordance with absolutely mystifying and absurd norms. In particular, the fact that a conservatoire appoints someone between the age of thirty and thirty-five who then remains there until the age of sixty-five or seventy is quite mad! Education should be a question of movement. The teacher should place himself on the same level as his students; he should test himself out and constantly vary his methods; he should even vary the end results of his teaching and try to advance as he goes along. He should not come with a completely dead curriculum referring only to the past, but should teach with reference to the present; and the past should be experienced in terms of the present, which is certainly not the case nowadays. As I see it, a teacher should be given a contract for from three to five years, so that he can follow the progress of some students for a certain time; after that he should be able to change course, since even those who start with the best intentions in the world come to be afflicted with the worst kind of sclerosis after a time: they are obliged to go over the same things year after year, and it has no further interest for them.

Everything finally comes to be seen in terms of examinations — a sort of police investigation into your ability to carry out one sort of work or another. In the long run examinations are totally irrelevant. That is why you see so many products of the music schools turning into dried fruit! — completely enclosed in a narrow conservatism and believing that because they found ways of existing in the music of the past they hold the key to the truth. Really, education ought to be totally directed in terms of the present; unless one combines education with experiment and invention — and the three are inextricably bound up with each other — then the result will be a total incapability of expression.

CD: You spend some of your time in the United States. Does not this principle of movement, of the 'circulation' of teachers, exist over there — at least in theory?

PB: It does exist in theory. But there too, if you have obtained a post in a university for instance, you are virtually immovable. Very few people decide to put themselves back on the open market for very long, primarily for social, family, or sometimes financial reasons. Very few people possess the desire to exist independently strongly enough to feel forced to alter the pattern of their lives, and to re-examine themselves even from a professional point of view. It would be very difficult to require this of everyone.

But without being so adventurous, some system of recycling should be set up, of renewing available knowledge and teachers, if education is to remain a vital force. In the field of science, for example, this sort of recycling is absolutely indispensable. Unless you are aware of recent research — I mean in medicine, mathematics, physics, and so on — you are completely out of touch with modern science. I am not trying to equate the teaching of music with the teaching of science, but when musical thought advances — and at present there is quite vigorous progress — then there is no reason why teachers should not keep abreast of the development of musical invention from year to year, to see what consequences it might have for instrumental playing, for ways of thinking about composition, and for all the phenomena which go to make up musical life. As long as education is not made, above all things, to exist in the present, then it will be terribly handicapped.

CD: Do you not think that what prevents teachers from 'putting themselves back on the open market' is possibly the lack of full employment in our society, which makes them afraid?

PB: Yes, and these economic factors I can well understand. Some-one, for instance, who has family responsibilities will think twice, and even three or four times, before re-examining his existence and putting his financial resources at risk. Sometimes, unwillingly, he may even turn his back on adventure for the sake of security. No one can be blamed for this, but if it were possible to maintain economic and social security and still have the possibility of renewing and to some extent varying teaching staff we should have an ideal solution. Of course ideal solutions are never the practical ones that are adopted; of this I am convinced from my own experience. But even without the ideal solution one can try to move towards it, because if no effort is ever made in this direction education will always lag behind as it does today.

CHAPTER VI
TOWARDS THE DISSOLUTION OF CLASSICAL FORMS
THE SECOND PIANO SONATA

CD: Let us now move on to your Second Piano Sonata. There is a vast difference between the First and the Second. In your conversations with Goléa[8] you say that here you broke with the dodecaphonic series and brought rhythmic imagination into play. However, a study of the work brings to light pitch sequences and relationships that recur in a constant manner and perhaps represent an underlying memory of this series.

PB: There is a great difference between the First and the Second Sonatas because in the meantime I had written a work (which I have since lost) that was in effect a transitional work. This being said, in the Second Sonata I only broke with the 'concept' of the Schoenbergian note-row. What attracted me in the manipulation of the twelve notes at that period was the idea of giving them a functional significance, a meaning as motifs and themes in relation to certain functions that they were to fulfil in the work.

This can be seen very easily in the first movement of my Second Sonata: series of intervals are associated with certain motifs and recur later; this series of notes is divided into a certain number of motifs which supply the material for the entire first movement in particular. I was also interested in a form of expression that would establish a contrast between a style based on thematic motifs and an athematic one; in other words, I think of the theme as an accumulation of possibilities, but at the same time for the development sections of this sonata movement I wanted gradually to dissolve the intervallic cells, to draw attention more to the rhythmic elaboration than to the intervals, whose function now is secondary. Interest should increase or diminish in relation to the actual structure of the motifs and of the intervals. The very strong, sharply-outlined thematic structures of the opening gradually dissolve in a development that is completely amorphous from this point of view, until they gradually return. The whole of the first movement is made up of this contrast between very precise motifs and their dissolution into imprecise intervals.

The second movement, on the other hand, is built on the

principle of the trope, of the large-scale variation. A fairly brief first section is established according to very obvious structural principles. A much longer second section is the trope of the first, and here certain figures and developments recur symmetrically. Certain motifs give rise to exactly the same kind of trope. This is a way of thinking to which I have become very attached, and which I have used again several times, particularly in a later work, the Third Piano Sonata. It involves taking a fairly simple text and causing it to proliferate by running in parallel certain elements of, let us say, type A, always varied and amplified in a given way, with elements of type B, so that the structure of the original simple text can be found again in the larger text, in a variation; but this variation will not be mechanical but truly organic, because it is itself an amplification of even the small motifs that went to make up the original text. Basically this text can be read on two levels: one very simple, the other much more complex. There is a divergence of opinion about the same text; a form that is peculiarly my own and which I tried out for the first time in this second movement.

The third movement is much more conventional. I tried to combine the variation form with the scherzo form. It was one of the last vestiges of classicism that still meant anything to me as far as form was concerned.

By contrast, the fourth movement is extremely free. It consists of two sections, one slow, the other extremely fast. The slow section is written in a sort of canonic fugal style which gradually disintegrates because its intervals become more and more complex (and here too there is the same endeavour as in the first movement: in other words the music starts out with a very obvious thematic texture and later becomes completely athematic). In the fast section there is once more a very marked use of motifs that is brought to an end by exploding all the cells, which then become indistinguishable one from another as they are reduced to their smallest constituent parts; so that it is impossible to associate these exploded fragments with any one motif rather than another.

It was probably the attempt of the Viennese school to revive older forms that made me try to destroy them completely: I mean I tried to destroy the first-movement sonata form, to disintegrate slow movement form by the use of the trope, and repetitive

41

scherzo form by the use of variation form, and finally, in the fourth movement, to demolish fugal and canonic form. Perhaps I am using too many negative terms, but the Second Sonata does have this explosive, disintegrating and dispersive character, and in spite of its own very restricting form the destruction of all these classical moulds was quite deliberate. After the Second Sonata I never again wrote with reference to a form belonging to the past. I have always found one that came with the idea of the work itself.

CHAPTER VII
ENCOUNTER WITH RENE CHAR

CD: This quality of explosiveness, this disintegration into a multitude of figurations that you have referred to in connection with the Second Piano Sonata, does it not equally characterise *Le Visage Nuptial?*

PB: Probably. Here I would draw a parallel with Schoenberg and Webern. The first version of *Le Visage Nuptial* is earlier than the Second Piano Sonata, but all the revision was done afterwards. The fact that I used a text compelled me to find a different form. In the central piece in particular, which is the longest, I made no attempt at all to impose a classical form on a text that did not require it. I split up the text according to its meaning, and of course I used parallel sequences that went with the meaning of the poem; but the form, too, adheres completely to the text itself. It is not at all classical, but refers to the poem while still retaining a sufficiently tight construction of its own not to be merely a kind of parody of the poem.

CD: Perhaps this is the moment to take a further look at your literary affinities, with particular reference to Char. Two of the works of your first period as well as the later *Le Marteau sans Maître* are based on poems by Char. Other interviewers – and I am thinking of Goléa – claim that you drew attention to the strain of violence in his poetry and declare that this was possibly what first attracted you to him.[9]

PB: What struck me in Char's poetry when I first discovered it (in late 1945 or 1946) was, in the first place, its condensation. It was as if I had discovered a worked flint: it had a sort of contained violence – not a violence expressed in gestures, but an internal violence, concentrated in a very tense manner of expression. This was the first thing that struck me about him, and it still strikes me now. What I found most attractive about Char was not what people call his 'love of Nature', his feeling for Provence or direct relationship with humanity, but rather his power to sum up his

43

world in an extremely concise form of expression, to exteriorise it and to fling it far away from him.

Since my ideas about setting a poem to music have little in common with the usual conceptions, I found that Char's condensation of the word was a great help from that point of view, too. If a text is too extended then time becomes so expanded that music can no longer have any *raison d'être* in relation to it. In Char's poetry, on the other hand, where time is extremely concentrated, music does not distend time but can be grafted onto it. Such a poem does not defy music, but rather invites it. So this is another way in which Char's poetry attracted me. In the three works *Le Visage Nuptial, Le Soleil des Eaux* and *Le Marteau sans Maître*, I was progressively reducing things: in other words, in *Le Visage Nuptial* the text is long whereas in *Le Marteau sans Maître* I chose the shortest poems, of just a few lines, which allowed me to have a completely different conception of the relation between poetry and music — no longer as a simple meeting between poetry and music, but as a graft in which music and poem still retain their independence up to a point.

CD: Did you at that time, or later, have any personal contact with Char?

PB: I met him in the summer of 1947, about a year after I had got to know his poetry. That was the beginning of a long friendship. Nowadays of course, with the rather chaotic existence I lead, and above all since I left France — nearly sixteen years ago — I have seen much less of him, and I regret this a great deal, for I am very attached to him, not only as a poet, but also as a man.

CD: Is there any correspondence between the man and his poetry? I mean, does knowing the man help one to understand his poetry?

PB: Certainly. I cannot separate his normal relaxed way of speaking from the way he speaks in his poems. In the first place he is a man of highly personal and striking vision; he has a way of saying things which corresponds to what he writes. Of course it is less condensed: what he writes has been worked on and elaborated; but his natural speech is already quite personal to him, and there is no hiatus between the spoken and the written word.

CD: Is there anything of the violence we find in the poems of which you were speaking just now in Char's view of the world?

PB: It is certainly a part of the man, but it should not be confused with contempt for the world. Contempt serves no useful purpose; but violence is a kind of dialectic of existence that makes it possible to progress.

CD: Do you think there is anything in common between this violence and that of Michaux?

PB: No, I don't think so. Michaux's 'violence' (and the word seems absurd) is less 'solar'. Char's violence belongs to the heat of the day — it has the power of the noonday sun. In Michaux, on the other hand, it is contained — it is the violence of dark vaults and caves. The two temperaments are diametrically opposed. I have known both men, and could sense that Char's personality had nothing in common with Michaux's. They are poles apart.

CD: We have talked about the integration of poem and music in *Le Visage Nuptial* and about the specially brief texts of *Le Marteau sans Maître*. I should think in this context *Le Soleil des Eaux* is a kind of parenthesis: the conceptual and semantic elements of the poem are thrown into greater relief. The text can be understood through the recitative, through the vocal line, which is not the case with the other works. Is this because the work started out as incidental music, or did you have a different viewpoint when you composed *Le Soleil des Eaux*?

PB: The viewpoint was different. I do not think the fact that the music was not written in direct relation to the poem had any great influence.

In fact, the first piece, a monody broken up by orchestral passages, was composed in two quite different stages: the monody was written as a piece to be sung in the radio adaptation of the play, but it was never sung in its entirety because it was much too long. The poem Char had given me was still unpublished. I conceived it in terms of a solo voice; and I thought it would be interesting, rather than trying to find an accompaniment, to articulate it by means of interjections, reflections, landscapes, and distorted images — a notion I had gained from writing some incidental music. Each of these interruptions is very different and very homogeneous: they have nothing in common with each other but are in

45

fact of distinctly contrasting types. Ultimately I conceived the piece as an antiphony between two existing things and their potential for coming together. It is a kind of functional collage in which the orchestral interjections are determined by the articulatory points in the melodic line. Obviously there is no reason why one should not understand the text if the singer articulates it well: it was intended as a continuous text to be declaimed in a very simple manner.

When it comes to the second movement, however, things begin to be more complex. I added orchestral passages which I fitted much more closely together because the various developments in the orchestra are truly organic: they are put together with reference to one another and create their own form. This time, I integrated the form into the poem so that — unlike the first poem, where the melodic line was written first — the melodic lines for the second poem were inspired by the orchestral textures. The entire choral part was added on and integrated completely with the orchestral structure. There is practically no autonomous choral structure. When I worked on the final version I made use of the ambiguity underlying a text spoken either collectively or individually. This interaction between collective and individual declamation is something I have often used, and it is an important element in my ideas about setting texts.

It should be borne in mind — and I drew attention to this with the quotation from Char which serves as preface to the score[10] — that these two particular texts represent a somewhat free-and-easy version of anguish and violence, and even of the formal discipline of language. In the context of Char's work they are very simple poems; there was no reason to compose very complex music for texts which themselves required only a simple presentation.

CD: In speaking of the works of Char we come to one of your personal tendencies, that of returning to earlier compositions and re-working them. In this respect you are at the opposite extreme from Stockhausen, who puts things behind him and admits that he never wants to go back to a previous work. Even if he considers he has made a terrible blunder, he prefers to try again in a different way. You, on the other hand, seem to be quite undaunted by the fatigue involved in going back to work on a piece you have already written.

46

PB: I am very much at the opposite extreme: as long as I am dissatisfied with something it lingers in my memory and I cannot get rid of it. It stays there permanently, and that is what compels me to go back to it.

In the particular case of *Le Soleil des Eaux* I was dissatisfied with the use of three soloists because the balance with the orchestra was not good. So I first set about rectifying the problem of the relative weight of the voices and the orchestra by amplifying the voices — in other words I rewrote the three solo and tutti passages. It was not very clever to try to solve the problem of balance simply by writing the words 'solo' or 'tutti' above a line that had originally been conceived as a solo, and when I returned to the work I saw that the problem lay deeper and that if I was to alternate between the individual and the collective I should have to go further and decide what could be said collectively and what ought to be said individually. This forced me to revise completely the choral writing in the second piece. The third version was made after the work had been performed a number of times. I was not at all satisfied with the orchestration, which I had done while I was very young and inexperienced, and which I later found awkward from the purely intrumental point of view and not really close enough to the text. What I needed was an orchestration that could go more deeply into the basic details of the text — that could illuminate them, and not just be conditioned by my own invention from one moment to the next. This invention itself needed to be related to the text at all times and to be completely adequate for it. So I revised the orchestration, bearing in mind firstly the need for the instrumentation to be adequate for the music itself and for the text, and secondly the need for an orchestration whose balance and timbres were more skilfully managed. This led me to rework the piece from top to bottom in different stages: it was not the musical text at all, but only its external aspect that I worked on. Now I am satisfied: the work is behind me, forgotten. From this angle it would no longer occur to me to revise it again.

Other works, however, are still in the making, since what is important to me is proliferation. As long as my ideas have not exhausted every possibility of proliferation they stay in my mind, and it is only when that has been completely achieved that I can get rid of them. This is probably a purely personal attitude.

CD: Here I am tempted to make a comparison with a writer you do not mention among your direct references: Proust. He too seems to have been very demanding about the final stages of his work.

PB: Yes. In French literature at any rate, there are two writers who bring this to mind: Proust and Mallarmé. I remember a letter from Mallarmé to his friend the poet Théodore Aubanel. Mallarmé, who was at that time living at Tournon, sent him a poem. His friend found some obscurities in it. Mallarmé then took back the text and revised it. A few months later, he sent the poem back to receive the following reply: 'As for the second version of your "Poëme nocturne", there are still some obscurities in the first part — some lines I cannot quite grasp. Is this my fault?' In fact, the more Mallarmé strove for clarity, the more obscure he became.[11] This is more or less what happens in such cases: the author in fact feels a need for clarity and self-evidence that will give his work depth, but at first sight it will become more obscure. His first shot at the work, the original version, will be an effort at clarity; only it will not seem sufficiently evident. In order to be more self-evident, you go deeper; but in effect, at a given moment, this quest for a self-evidence becomes a barrier to direct understanding. But I approve of the quest: I like a work that will bear several readings.

CHAPTER VIII
CONVERGENCE WITH MALLARME
LIVRE FOR STRING QUARTET

CD: You often return works to the drawing board, but even so it seems that some of them have been written at one go: for instance, your Second Piano Sonata, *Le Marteau sans Maître* and the *Livre* for string quartet, about which I should like to speak now. There are two versions of the work, but intentionally so, the one not eliminating the other.

PB: Exactly. When I re-read the String Quartet, which had long since been finished, I saw that it posed great interpretative problems for a quartet, and that you would need a conductor to solve them. Now it would hardly be very convincing to have a conductor for a string quartet; and so, having played the transcription of Webern's Five Movements op. 5 a number of times, I felt that the best way of bringing out everything in the original composition would be to orchestrate it. But in an orchestral work one can no longer have the same point of view; so I rethought the music completely, and in the two movements of the *Livre* for string quartet that became a *Livre* for string orchestra (basically the music is the same) there is such a degree of proliferation, and such an additional weight of ideas, that it is almost a new piece. In this matter I am like some nineteenth-century painters – Cézanne, for instance, who kept returning to the motif of the Mont Sainte-Victoire. Why did he keep coming back to it? Why did he need to return to it twenty or thirty times? Probably because there are things you come back to in order to fix your horizon in relation to yourself – to see where you stand. In my case it is a kind of revision demanded by a form that is capable of offering more.

CD: It was during the early stages of writing this string quartet that you first began to think about the possibility of generalising the note-row.

PB: Particularly in the last movement, as there was an inventive coincidence there, I began by using completely independent schemes in which pitches, durations and rhythms were combined

49

at first starting from cells, but these cells became so independent that they virtually became rhythmic series. In order to bring out these rhythmic series I found I was obliged to create series of dynamics. Gradually I found myself confronted with the following problem: how could I reconcile my decisions about the pitches — in other words the notes themselves — with my invention of the rest? I needed to find a technique that would go with the technique of pitches. This is how progressively I began to think about the generalisation of serial technique, though it was still bound up with the invention of motifs and cells, as can be seen very plainly in the last movement of the quartet.

CD: The title of the work is *Livre* — 'book'. This is something that should be underlined. For a long time you have wanted to write works that would be true books. You have not always been able to hold to this initial intention, but perhaps you still mean to do so? At any rate, would it be correct to say that you still have this tendency to think in terms of large-scale works either allowing some degree of selection or occupying an entire concert, as was to be the case with *Pli selon Pli*? What are your reasons for this?

PB: I believe in it more and more; the more I go on, the more I try to unify certain aspects of invention. All the works I write are basically different facets of one central work, of one central concept. In any case I cannot easily detach myself from a particular musical universe; once I have set it in motion it has a tendency to become independent and to grow. Unfortunately, circumstances sometimes prevent me from expanding it sufficiently, and this is why there are still 'expanding universes' that have not reached a completed state. I cannot bring myself to let go of material that is still alive for me. The same thing happened with *Eclat*, which began as a very small piece: in its present state it lasts twenty-five minutes. I have now composed a great deal more — about twice as much — and next time I shall play it in its entirety.

CD: This central conception that you refer to, is it not rather like Mallarmé's idea of 'Livre'? Yet very little was known about Mallarmé's *Livre* when you wrote this string quartet, so there can have been no direct reference; even so, the coincidence is rather striking.

PB: To be accurate I shall have to quote dates. This idea of a

Livre for string quartet, which, right from the start, was to be made up of detachable movements, came to me in 1948/49, probably while reading *Igitur* and *Le Coup de Dés*. I had found that the poem was no longer an isolated fragment, but that it might be part of a wide continuity as well as of one that could be broken up: in other words, a continuity from which sections could be detached because they had meaning and validity even when taken out of the continuous context in which they were placed. That is what interested me.

When I wrote my Third Piano Sonata much later, in 1956/57, I had still not read Mallarmé's *Livre* as it was not published until the end of 1957. I had called one of the work's formants 'Constellation', and I was asked if I had read this unpublished work of Mallarmé. 'No', I replied: 'where can I get hold of it?' I read it afterwards and found that the way I had conceived the Third Sonata, without of course being identical, was very close to Mallarmé's conception of the 'open book', and in particular his idea of the three-dimensional book — that is, where the developments become more and more complex as one moves into further dimensions of the content. One of the formants of this sonata is based on this principle. For the time being I have put it on ice as I want to work on it more, but this is a conception that is very much part of my thinking. As you get deeper into a book there ought to be a more or less complex texture because you have gradually been accumulating knowledge; in other words, you do not read page 1 in the same way as page 30. Page 1 is simple, whereas page 30 is complex because it contains all the knowledge you have gained from pages 1 to 29. This is what I sometimes do in music; developments accumulate and become tropes grafted on to other tropes, which in turn are superimposed on yet other tropes so that one gets different accumulations of richness. For me this represents a very special procedure: this accumulation that springs from a very simple principle, to end in a chaotic situation because it is engendered by material that turns in on itself and becomes so complex that it loses its individual shape and becomes part of a vast chaos.

I also like to create a contrast between structures that are extremely clear and those that are so overloaded that they cannot possibly be assimilated. In a passage that is obvious, simple and

51

clear, you assimilate a hundred per cent of what is said because all the articulations can be easily distinguished – the direction of the music, its general form, and so on. On the other hand, in an extremely complex passage the superimpositions are sometimes so dense that they cancel each other out, and ultimately give only an overall impression. This contrast between really total perception and an overall perception where details are lost is one of the things that mean most to me. For me, it is also related to a conception of time in general: in a very clear structure, time is very leisurely and there is time to hear everything; in an accumulation, on the other hand, the global time cannot be broken down. A lot of this I discovered as I went along, but I already had a broad awareness of the available options at the time of the *Livre* for string quartet.

CD: We have here reached a point where several paths meet. This notion of time, this proliferation of works from a single 'global' work is obviously the path that links you most directly with Mallarmé, and perhaps also with Proust; yet doesn't it also link Proust, Mallarmé and yourself with Wagner?

PB: Without any doubt! There was a great deal of astonishment when I accepted an invitation to conduct Wagner. He is a composer who has greatly impressed me with his feeling for large-scale organisation in which one can move from one point to another, passing through very varied landscapes. One of the most decisive features in Wagner, more so even than his musical language, is this constant reference of all the sections of a work to a central core. It is a conception that he stressed and there is no doubt that behind the literary influences it is the influence of Wagner that is at the root of my own project.

CD: And perhaps this is also what those writers admired in Wagner?

PB: I think so – especially in the case of someone like Mallarmé, but even for Proust too: I am thinking of the passage in which Proust describes the third act of *Tristan und Isolde*[12]. He points out that Wagner constructs the entire scene from that simple shepherd's tune heard on a single monodic instrument and that this motif eventually holds together the whole of the first scene of the third act. This description suggests that Proust completely understood how Wagner worked, never going back on himself

52

but always using the same motifs, the same basic resources, in order to achieve a continuous development that is both extremely concise and extremely free. This passage in Proust on the third act of *Tristan* is one of the most impressive things ever written about Wagner. Unfortunately it is also one of the least well known. Albertine is away for the afternoon, having gone to the theatre, and the author gives us his reflections on the construction of Wagner's musical continuity.

CD: I am now going to talk in a way I detest: that is, behave like those critics who take personal impressions as a basis for objective judgments.

I have always been struck by the austerity of the *Livre* for string quartet. If this is not too subjective a criterion (and that is why I ask), is it to be attributed to the serial treatment, even to the very essence of the series, or else to the homogeneity of its timbres? Or did you yourself not feel it?

PB: There are austere movements, but this is primarily because I was very preoccupied with problems of technique relating to expression. Furthermore, the natural violence of my piano writing as exemplified in the Second Sonata disappears here because the string quartet is neither a violent nor a noisy instrument. The mere fact of using a string quartet brought with it a certain reticence, a certain restraint. In some of the movements there is the austerity of research itself, which compelled me to limit the possible ways of using phrases, motifs and so forth. But particularly in the slow movements (which were played once or twice in Darmstadt by the Hamann Quartet) there are, in contrast, moments of great activity — decorative passages of great exuberance, even baroque in character. I hope my orchestration will bring this out.

So there is a contrast between the 'austere' movements, as you call them, which are somewhat rough-edged even within this austerity, and other relatively supple and flexible movements. This oscillation between the austerity of some passages that are deliberately stripped to their essentials, rigid even, and the flexibility of other movements or passages based on very profuse melismata and supple rhythmic structures that give permanent flexibility and a quasi-improvisatory style, makes a contrast that is fundamental to me. In certain passages of my scores you will often find the direction 'il faut comme improviser' (to be played as if improvised), that is to say there should be no feeling of the work that has gone into getting things right, but rather of communicating an impression of flexibility and improvisation. On the other hand, you will also find 'tempo strict', for instance, or 'strict dans les relations rythmiques' ('the rhythmic relations are to be strictly maintained') wherever structural rigidity is required and should have its full weight. There is a double polarity because sometimes the music reveals its bare bones while at other times the whole structure is concealed beneath a much more flexible, much more fragile covering.

CHAPTER IX
THE EXPANSION OF SERIAL TECHNIQUE
A WORLD OF EXPERIMENTS

CD: Your first book of *Structures* for two pianos was composed shortly before the appearance of your article 'Eventuellement'[13], which reflected the experience you had gained in composing *Structures* and *Polyphonie X*. 'Eventuellement' was followed two years later by a further article called 'Recherches maintenant'[14] which read like a disavowal of those who had been too thorough or too prompt in falling into step, and perhaps also like an exercise in self-criticism. It is curious, however, that *Structures* begins with a statement of its material, when you had rejected the mechanics of Webernian serialism.

PB: What I attempted there was what Barthes might call a reduction of style to the degree zero. By way of incidental background I might mention that I wanted to give the first *Structure* in particular — a piece composed as early as 1951 — the title of a painting by Klee, 'At the limit of the fertile land'. This painting is mainly constructed on horizontal lines with a few oblique ones, so that it is very restricted in its invention. The first *Structure* was quite consciously composed in an analogous way. It is equally incidental to mention the circumstances of its composition, but the first piece was written very rapidly, in a single night, because I wanted to use the potential of a given material to find out how far automatism in musical relationships would go, with individual invention appearing only in some really very simple forms of disposition — in the matter of densities, for example. For this purpose I borrowed material from Messiaen's *Mode de Valeurs et d'Intensités*; thus I had material that I had not invented and for whose invention I deliberately rejected all responsibility in order to see just how far it was possible to go. I wrote down all the transpositions, as though it were a mechanical object which moved in every direction, and I limited my role to the selection of registers — but even those were completely undifferentiated. The distribution is statistically the same in each of the small structures that make up the first piece; only the denisty varies, because after all some formal development was necessary. I chose a range of densities from one to six — in fact the most ordinary imaginable — in order to find all the densities that could be obtained between a single part and a superimposition of six parts. For me it was an experiment in what one might call Cartesian doubt: to bring everything into question again, make a clean sweep of one's heritage and start all over again from scratch, to see how it might be possible to reconstitute a way of writing that begins with something which eliminates personal invention.

In *Structures* you can follow the process of re-introducing personal invention; it is very clear, though not perhaps to everyone because I later deliberately muddled things by not printing the pieces in chronological order, so as to give an anti-evolutionary impression of the whole. So the first piece is purely automatic; the second already introduces a certain regularity: there is no longer just this statistical feature of twelve values, but polarisations centering on certain points in the series; these become rhythmically regular and so already establish a certain sense of direction in the midst of this statistically-differentiated world. After this, the third piece is very strongly directed towards oppositions between completely static passages and frenetically dense ones. Despite the conception of the basic material, which is still very inflexible, there is already that contrast, which to my mind is necessary to composition, between the will to make something out of the material and what the material itself suggests to one. In short, I gradually moved from the point where the material suggested itself to me until the situation was reversed: at the end of the second piece it was in fact I who was suggesting to the material that we make something together. This piece was very important in my development. I composed it relatively quickly, in perhaps a month and a half. What interested me was to see how the 'material/myself' relationship was gradually reversed to become 'myself/material', so that afterwards I was completely free of complexes about the strict organisation of one's material. I had taken the experience to absurd lengths, and it is very amusing that certain commentators, even those who are themselves composers, have failed to see this element of absurdity in the undertaking. I had made it perfectly clear from the start by choosing someone else's material. Thus this sort of absurdity, of chaos and mechanical wheels-within-wheels tending almost towards the random, was completely intentional and has probably been one of my most fundamental experiments as a composer. But I was very conscious of making it right from the start. At that point disorder is equivalent to an excess of order and an excess of order reverts to disorder. The general theme of this piece is really the ambiguity of a surfeit of order being equivalent to disorder. This equivalence between disorder and order is finally overthrown, becoming an opposition between the two.

CD: This is the point at which to put a question that might well be asked nowadays by people who are specially concerned with semiotics. What you have just said was principally concerned with the genesis of the work. The result of this genesis is obviously very plain in the piece you describe as 'automatic'. It is much less plain when one comes to analyse the other two pieces. Do you think that an *a posteriori* analysis knowing nothing about all this could still reveal the genesis of the work? In other words, can *Structures* be analysed in the same way as any other work?

PB: No, because where it is most analysable it is least differentiated, and where it is least analysable it is most differentiated. This kind of contrary relation between procedure and result has been one of my fundamental preoccupations because, as I have just said, where the material is clear but undifferentiated it is perfectly and easily analysable; then where the material is broken up and elaborated it becomes progressively more impossible to analyse. Moreover, from the analytical point of view, it is not a very interesting thing to try. Later, however, in my next work, my aim was to create a material that would be clear and analysable other than through the twelve notes of the series; a material, too, which would at all times take into account the music itself and would resolve the discrepancy between clarity of analysis and clarity of expression.

CD: When I spoke of analysis, I was not thinking of an exclusively morphological type of analysis. What I wanted to find out was whether it was possible to achieve a satisfactory analysis from the syntactical point of view. Obviously what happens at the genetical level at a certain moment is no longer of interest to anyone; it will concern you alone.

PB: Exactly. From the formal point of view, the second piece is easy to analyse since it consists of very long, static passages with almost no activity, alternating with active passages that are at first relatively complex and then amplified and superimposed on each other to produce extremely dense textures in which the listener will lose his way completely. Later these textures thin out again a great deal and end up by being quite simple. It is a kind of bell-shaped arc that is very easy to grasp.

CD: After the *Structures* for two pianos came *Polyphonie X*. This served as a work of reference for many musicians in 1953. I remember that it was often heard at Darmstadt alongside Stockhausen's *Kontrapunkte*. The explanations published at that time in your article 'Eventuellement' give some idea of what the idea of X might imply – namely, a sort of diagonal projection of the series. It would seem that you have to some extent repudiated this work: in any case it has not been heard since. Just where do things stand with regard to it?

PB: I have not repudiated it, because there was nothing to repudiate; but it is a work which simply shows the inadequate education I had had at the time. You must know that classes at the Conservatoire put little emphasis on instrumental education proper. But the more you advance, the more you need to be sure of what you are doing in this respect.

I wrote *Polyphonie* between the first piece of *Structures* and the two others. It was an intermediate work and suffers from theoretical exaggeration; it is not that I need a theory in order to function, but it remains true that for ideas to be communicated they require an absolutely perfect and flexible technique. At that particular time, however, I was looking for a technique. In fact the work is based on total serialisation, but also on rhythmic cells, and this very rigid organisation prevented me from concentrating on the instrumental side. It is rather a sort of abstract blueprint: the instruments are only there to play the notes according to whether they belong to one register or another. (This kind of conception naturally works on the piano because in order to hit a note there is no great need to worry about pianistic technique. Moreover, it was more natural for me to turn to the piano as it was my own instrument.) Apart from the quality of timbre – in other words the combinations of instruments themselves — there is nothing in the writing of *Polyphonie* that takes account of instrumental capacities and potential as such: the instrumental groups are selected for their abstract values in combination, which is not the ideal approach and is what caused me to hold this work in reserve. One day I shall probably take it up again, though I don't know when, as it would need fundamental rethinking of the problem of communicating musical ideas of this sort by means of an instrumental ensemble. It would also need a vast number of new ideas to diversify the work's developments. I have not wanted it to be played again because it is certainly very awkward and rigid.

CD: It is no part of your way of thinking to conceive of art as being something constantly in the making, as Stockhausen once defined it [15]. With you, on the contrary, what is important is the finished work. Even if one thinks that, from the genetical point of view, techniques are extremely interesting — the manipulation of the series, for instance — and that they constitute a necessary stage, it is nonetheless true that what survives is the finished object. What is your attitude towards the very fertile but also very experimental period we have been discussing, in terms of its aesthetic results?

PB: I think that no work can be valid when its technique is not flexible enough or has become such a major concern that it gets in the way of aesthetic considerations. It can only become valid when technical preoccupations are transformed into an aesthetic aim — into 'expression', to use the simple word and avoid jargon. As long as expression is held back, halted or paralysed by an inflexible technique that is itself trying to work out its identity, the work will not be satisfactory. I have often said that pre-occupation with technique and preoccupation with aesthetics are like two mirrors. Invention passes from one to the other like an image that is perpetually reflected between two parallel mirrors. This is why I absolutely insist that the two mirrors should be present, should be in parallel, and should have equal importance. Regarding most of the works that were composed at that period, I feel only that they were projects that satisfied me from an intellectual point of view: there is a kind of dichotomy between the mental project, the abstract plan, the intellectual satisfaction, even the satisfaction of manipulating things, and the final result. Manipulation is all-important, but it must be a technical tool, an intermediary. To cut a window pane you need a diamond, but the diamond itself is of no importance if you think of it simply as a diamond. I think that during that particular period there was too great a tendency in general, and certainly on my part, to cut the facets of the diamond without bothering too much about how well it would cut glass, or even whether it would do the job at all. This period was fairly short-lived as far as I was concerned, because I have always been conscious of the necessity for music to be essentially communicative; all the same, I have not lost sight of the fact that this kind of theoretical asceticism and the tough, sometimes arduous work involved brought with it many discoveries; only now, the more I go on, the more I feel that technical considerations are subordinate to the expression I want to convey, and not just a search for method. But at that period there was uncertainty about the evolution of music, and it was not possible to do otherwise. Musical methodology had to be questioned, and it is quite certain that the fact of changing these methods, finding new ones, and using them in different ways, tended to push the real aims of the work into the background. Whatever else may be said for it, I do not find that an advantage.

CD: Regarded in this way, did the composer not become something of a research scientist at that time?

PB: I should think that research scientists are a lot less speculative, in the bad sense of the word — that is, they are less liable to be hypnotised by a construction that may satisfy them from the intellectual point of view. The real research workers are precisely those who are constantly in touch with reality, and who modify their working hypotheses according to their findings. The pseudo-scientist, on the other hand, will invent a construction for his own satisfaction without being too concerned about relating it to reality: reality is in error when it does not agree with his construction. In general, the true spirit of research, whatever field one works in, is a continual interaction between the reality one has to take into account and the system of hypotheses one must apply to it. This constant interchange ought always to be present in our thinking, and in my opinion nothing could be more fruitful than this perpetual modification of perspective, of hypotheses, in the face of musical reality.

CD: I made that comparison because it is impossible not to be aware that there exists, nevertheless, a tendency in science, especially in theoretical physics (Heisenberg, de Broglie, etc), for theoretical hypothesis rather than experiment to become the starting-point for the establishment of a system.

PB: I am really not in a position to discuss scientific points of view, but it is certainly true that Heisenberg, de Broglie — indeed all scientists who have made fundamental discoveries in modern times — have put forward hypotheses. This is quite logical: first you put forward a hypothesis, and then you find out whether it can be verified later. Intuition plays a much greater part than is generally believed. It is often thought that scientists are simply people who deduce consequences from the results of their experiments in a fairly logical fashion, and gradually arrive at a conclusion. In point of fact, however, as is shown in the particular cases you have just quoted, although the scientific mind does make deductions from observations, at a given moment it will also be open to a phenomenon of an almost irrational kind that will still be a deduction but an intuitive one. This can be seen not only in the field of science but in all the expressive media too. Of course, the ground has to be prepared, for there is nothing accidental about intuition; but when the ground has been prepared for intuition, when every possible conclusion has been drawn from the facts, then comes the hypothesis that is almost entirely intuitive. There is an illuminating interplay between the hypothesis and the previously-prepared ground. At a certain moment there is no longer a kind of chain of deductions, but rather a break — perhaps even quite a violent break — and this is the moment of intuition. Afterwards the chain can be mended in retrospect by returning to the phenomena one was studying before. This procedure is fundamental to human thought, and to creative thought in particular. Usually when a discovery is made it is the result of a discontinuity of thought; very seldom does continuity of thought lead to a discovery.

CD: What about the future of the works dating from this period?

Since they were primarily of interest from the genetical point of view, ought they still to be played?

PB: Certainly. A work such as my *Structures* for two pianos, for instance, can still undoubtedly be played as a document, because there is no instrumental problem here and the compositional problem is solved more satisfactorily than in *Polyphonie*. The latter, moreover, is a later work and the reason I have withdrawn it is precisely because the compositional technique itself was not thought through.

CD: Are there any precedents in the history of music for a work to be heard as a document?

PB: I think not, unless we go back to the music of the Middle Ages. There was never the same enormous theoretical effort when they were trying to codify certain polyphonic practices. And things were not the same in the eighteenth century either. In our own times there has certainly been this malaise, so to speak, although it was dispersed very quickly. A crisis that lasts two or three years is not really very long. There was a transitional period, rather like a tunnel you have to go through to get to the other side of a mountain; it took a few years to get through that tunnel, years during which theoretical endeavour was such that research and composition became incompatible.

CD: In fact, the importance of this transitional period will gradually diminish as we get further away from it, but at that time it was of undoubted importance for those who lived through it.

CHAPTER X
TOWARDS A NEW RHETORIC
LE MARTEAU SANS MAITRE

CD: I mentioned just now that everyone used to listen to the recording of *Polyphonie* at Darmstadt. Many composers latched on to it as on to a comfortable bandwagon; others, however, took the work, and also your article 'Eventuellement', as a starting-point for a serious and rigorous programme of research.

But then a year later, the *Nouvelle Revue Française* published an article no less resounding than 'Eventuellement', but in a completely opposite direction: 'Recherches maintenant'[16]. Many composers saw this as a check, making nonsense of their work, their experiments and their research. My own reaction was the immediate sensing of an exercise in self-criticism accompanied by new proposals which seemed to announce forthcoming developments in your own work. What was the truth of it all?

PB: I was certainly dissatisfied with the sort of inflexibility that had begun to characterise musical ideas. Invention is something that is essentially flexible, something that ought to be preserved for its independence and its flexibility. It should be always at one's command, and this was certainly not possible with the rigid intellectual structures that were inseparable from musical technique at that time. Furthermore, where organisations were pursued into such an abundance of detail one got into a situation of total absurdity because the accumulation of things that were dependent on different hierarchies meant that one was trying to organise a chaotic situation: this may be interesting as an extreme case but not as a basic phenomenon. An extreme case ought to remain an extreme case, and any such proliferation of theoretical abstractions removed from the realm of perception is unsatisfactory. In reality, what has to be taken into account before all else is the sensitive and sensory perception of phenomena. I see no great difference between the academicism of invertible counterpoint in six or eighteen parts that has no justification in aesthetical and musical terms, and an accumulation of series and serial laws on six or eight different levels. The problem is exactly the same: it is, in fact, a problem of academicism. As you said just now, it is very easy to be satisfied simply with organisations that provide a certain security, and to find them perfect because they obey certain numerical laws.

What I was denouncing was this fetishism of numbers and of numerical structures in general. It was a convenient fetishism, but no different from the Golden Section to which all proportions were supposed to be related. In the long run these things are all extremely banal. I have sometimes seen composers trying to describe their native country – seen it quite plainly in chapter and verse – and claiming that they could only keep in tune with their country's music by describing its mountains with a melodic curve. This is an even more vulgar type of fetishism, though of the same order. What it boils down to is trying to protect yourself in composition by using an order of reference which is supposedly infallible and which therefore guarantees your own infallibility.

I reacted pretty violently against this kind of thing, and I was quite right to do so since it was a completely sterile cul-de-sac. Some of the concerts at Darmstadt in 1953/54 were of quite lunatic sterility and academicism, and above all became totally uninteresting. One could sense the disparity between what was written and what was heard: there was no sonic imagination, but simply an accumulation of numerical transcriptions quite devoid of any aesthetic character.

CD: A great deal of your reasoning propounds something that seems permanent in your case: the dialectical character of your thought and attitudes, which causes you to move between rational and irrational poles. You have mentioned 'hysteria according to Artaud'[17]; you have given vent to irrational desires, and also spoken of 'delirium'[18], though stressing at the same time that 'it must be organised'. In your search for a new 'poetics' you feel the need to have a considerable technical apparatus in the background; your development constantly takes you from one pole to the other.

PB: I have the sort of temperament that tries to invent rules so as to have the pleasure of destroying them later: it is a dialectical evolution between freedom of invention and the need for discipline in invention. The two are inseparable: invention without discipline is very often inept, in the literal sense of the word; but discipline without invention is no less inept, since it is not applied to anything. The difficulty is to find a point of balance, or at least a constant interchange, between these extremes. You have to contribute your own element of irrationality while transcribing it in a rational way that alone can present the irrational potential you have within you. This irrational factor has to be put down in rational terms so that it can be reconstituted by others, who will in their turn make use of it to express their own irrational powers.

Notation is a fundamental feature in music, one that is based on rational and technical criteria. It is a tabulation, a code for communicating with other people — performers, fellow composers, or simply people who read scores. This code is a basis, a language for communication — only it is charged with elements which, whilst not destroying it, nevertheless modify it and lend it a multitude of inflections. The code of a great work is itself sufficiently flexible to sustain an irrational, emotional and affective interpretation that may completely transform it and make something interesting of it. If the code simply remains a code there will be no more emotion there than in the transmission of a telegram. In a normal code the irrational element does not appear at all — the phenomenon is entirely rational. But in the musical code such as we know it today the irrational is always grafted on to the rational. In fact the composer himself is tempted to express the inexpressible by means of extremely refined techniques that will enable him to graft a whole variety of related structures on to his own project. That is why this project must be extremely elaborate, perfect to a degree, so that it has this immense potential for additional superstructures. By contrast, with improvisations, because they are purely affective phenomena, there is not the slightest scope for anyone else to join in. Improvisation is a personal psychodrama, and is regarded as such. Whether we are interested or not, we cannot graft our own affective, intellectual or personal structure on to a base of this sort. This is proof *ab absurdo* that a work is delimited and justified in so far as it is a finite framework that can serve as a pretext for infinite proliferation.

CD: The work that best illustrates this way of going about things, once you had come through that dark period, is undoubtedly *Le Marteau sans Maître*. Here you invented new compositional procedures.

PB: Yes; although it is much easier to understand, and more attractive than the first book of *Structures* or *Polyphonie*, its technique is much more elaborate and skilful. It takes account of affective phenomena associated with music. For this reason the technique had to be infinitely more supple and lend itself to all kinds of invention. A technical analysis of *Le Marteau sans Maître* would certainly be very much more difficult than one of *Polyphonie*. There is in fact a very clear and very strict element of control, but starting from this strict control and the work's overall discipline there is also room for what I call *local indiscipline*: at the overall level there is discipline and control, at the local level there is an element of indiscipline — a freedom to choose, to decide and to reject.

In my previous works the strict and inflexible framework offered practically no possibility of rejection. But composition is a positive act, though a positive act made up of an accumulation of determining rejections. During the previous period no one wanted to reject anything but to bring everything into play at each moment. In *Le Marteau sans Maître*, which came immediately afterwards, I adopted a point of view that was not the opposite, but much more flexible: I was able to eliminate certain factors at a given moment in the composition, and it is precisely this negative aspect that gives a work liveliness: suddenly the pieces became individualised where otherwise there would be an undifferentiated overall structure. In *Le Marteau sans Maître* there is a highly differentiated structure arising from many positive aspects, but also from the element of rejection it imposes.

CD: In the 1954 article we were referring to, and which heralded *Le Marteau sans Maître*, there is a mention of a type of writing that might ultimately be able to embrace italics and parentheses. Are these simply literary images, or metaphors? If not, what would the musical equivalents be in concrete terms?

PB: This is an idea I first had in 1954, but it was not realized until my Third Piano Sonata of 1956/57, where certain external, linguistic or typographical features became a major preoccupation.

I had always been struck by the one-dimensional nature of music. Until then a musical work had a beginning and an end and you went from one to the other in a single stretch that was impossible to modify. From that time on I began to think about developments and sequences that could be modified. This is why in *Le Marteau sans Maître* — I have said this before, but it is important to stress it — there are three cycles based on three different poems. These three poems give rise to different pieces: one cycle contains three pieces, another two, and the last contains four. But instead of presenting these separate cycles one after the other, as they were composed, I arranged them so that they would interlock. Here was already an attempt to open up a further musical dimension. Each piece forms part of a cycle; that cycle is interrupted by another; I wanted to demonstrate a definite preoccupation with a further dimension permeating the organisation of the work. The fact that there is not just one continuity but several, that the cycles interpenetrate one another and that, in the last piece, they do so within a single piece (which is a microcosm of the entire work) marks an important stage in my progress towards what was effectively the breaking-up of musical continuity.

Much later I developed this idea by transforming the conception of homogeneity and non-homogeneity. For me, musical works had always been extremely homogeneous in time, but what I was looking for more and more was a discontinuity and non-homogeneity in musical material: very large and very long developments given to a specific texture which could be halted by a very rarefied texture that would imply a further dimension in time. I once said, in a joking way, that I would like sometimes to alternate Bruckner and Webern.

As for the instrumentation of *Le Marteau sans Maître*, the ensemble it uses (viola, alto flute, guitar, xylophone, vibraphone and percussion) now seems banal because it, or at any rate something like it (for it coloured all the ensembles that followed), has been used thousands of times; but it was the first of its kind. Up to that point I had used a virtually classical type of instrumentation, following the European tradition. Here for the first time I wanted to show the influence of non-European cultures, to which I had always been attracted. For the first time, too, I made greater allowances for the problems of instrumental playing and made the maximum use of each instrument's potential. In the two or three years that separate *Polyphonie* from *Le Marteau sans Maître* my preoccupations changed, above all in my investigations into instrumentation, which I found more and more exciting. Furthermore, this coincided with the beginning of the *Domaine musical* concerts, which brought me into continuous contact not just with instrumental problems – these I had always known, since I had worked with instrumentalists at the Théâtre Marigny – but, for the first time, with performers of contemporary music. This direct contact made me acutely aware of all the problems and all the resources of instrumentation.

CD: The changes which appeared in the form and the composition of *Le Marteau sans Maître* also brought with them considerable changes in notation, compared with the preceding period.

PB: In this work the notation does not go beyond the traditional limits; it is simply more complex. What struck me most at the time was not so much the notation itself as changes in tempo. In some pieces, in particular, the tempo was constantly being modified – there was no conception of a fixed tempo. I had been led to this type of mobility by certain very specific considerations. When I was working on my *Structures* for two pianos I was looking for rhythms and superpositions that would be extremely complex and yet precise. In the first draft – which has never been seen, because there was a second version immediately before publication – I had piled up ratios of 24:25, or 27:28, in other words, values so close together that it would be impossible to play them accurately. This was a bad way of presenting the problem in instrumental music. The procedure is valid for music on tape, since it is possible to cut the tape into the number of centimetres equivalent to the ratios one wants: it can be mechanically controlled. But no performer could play 28 against 27 without some precision mechanism implanted in his brain that would enable him to avoid the human error that would otherwise be one-hundred-per-cent certain.

Since this sort of writing inevitably gives rise to error, it was obviously better to try less complex rhythms that the performer could be one-hundred-per-cent sure of playing right, and modify them in some other way. Here, I reflected for the first time upon the fact that the definition of tempo that I had been taught earlier, even in Messiaen's classes, had nothing to offer in this respect. Tempo is the result both of a written numerical value and of the speed with which it is realized, which can completely change it. Bearing this in mind, it was much easier to obtain extremely complex relationships by writing ratios that were intrinsically simpler and introducing modifications in the speed of these numerical ratios or durational relationships. This gave me the idea, not of changing the notation – I had no urgent need to – but, on the contrary, of making use of this notation and adding indications of speed that would yield complex phenomena which would otherwise have eluded me.

In another piece – the ideas came to me at about the same time – I saw that it was possible to abolish completely all idea of speed in the real sense of the word, and even all numerical ideas, by piling up obstacles. If one introduces into a structure of fairly simple rhythms accumulations of grace notes that cause the tempo to be interrupted the whole time, one completely loses the idea of speed. The temporal aspect of my writing makes play of this inter-relationship between numerical values (seen as the basic phenomenon) and speed, which will modify the values by introducing into the actual writing material obstacles which by degrees lead to a loss of control in performance: activities so complicated and close together that they wipe out all reference to a pulsation. From then on I understood something that I later defined much more clearly. Musical time, which is the way in which we experience all musical events, may be felt as being 'pulsed', regularly or irregularly. This phenomenon is communicated in writing by obvious means – for instance, harmonic stresses, types of more or less deliberate repetition, and so forth. But there is also a kind of music that can do entirely without pulsations – a music that seems to float, and in which the writing itself makes it impossible for the performer to keep in line with a pulsed tempo: grace notes, ornaments, or a profusion of differences in dynamics will make the performer give so much attention to what is happening that temporal control recedes into the background. At such times the activity itself is more important than its control, so that at times mensural notation is no more than a visual aid. Such notation will not be respected because it can't be.

CD: We can relate these ideas to an article you wrote on the subject of electronic music, 'A la limite du pays fertile'[19]. Here, although you refer to the nature of tempo, you leave the question partly unresolved. Then you contrast the tempo of instrumental music with the non-tempo of electronic music, where the durations can always be measured in lengths of tape. Could one not conceive of tempo as being ultimately a peculiarly human factor which modifies agogics whilst ensuring some regulation of temporal relationships?

PB: In actual fact, even in electronic or electro-acoustical music where durational relationships are calculated, the human ear automatically supplies its own tempo, because this is a psychological factor. Just as, visually, we try to refer what we see to a unity of vision in order to assess it, when we hear something – even if it is something completely undifferentiated like the sounds of everyday life – we relate it to a unity so that we can measure and assess it. In this, our ear functions as an instrument for measuring time.

It is not possible to introduce phenomena of tempo into music that has been calculated only electronically, in terms of segments of time – lengths expressed in seconds or microseconds, and so on. Here one cannot speak of tempo because the modifications are imperceptible; there is always a calculation of duration which introduces a completely different relationship with musical time. What you can do is to introduce textural densities in a different way – for example, phenomena of longer or shorter periodicity or other factors that will provide a different way of conceiving time for each work or each moment of a work. But here too we shall no longer be dealing with what is generally called tempo, because tempo is a psychophysiological conception that is difficult to express simply in terms of figures. If, for instance, we were to analyse a pianist's *rubato*, even in familiar music (the word *rubato* is always linked with the name of Chopin), it would be interesting to calculate the exact durations in terms of some scale or other – perhaps a series of *rubato* semiquavers – and to see how this *rubato* is related to harmonic or melodic functions. We should find that the nuances were so delicate and so fleeting that it would be impossible to play them twice in exactly the same way; it is a category that eludes measurement. To make a true *rubato* on tape you would have to programme the machine so that at each replay it would produce different characteristics of time. The concept of tempo is a concept of 'error'. You deliberately make a mistake in the numerical data, and that is what introduces the idea of psychological tempo. If you try to introduce the idea of error artificially into a machine it will produce fixed errors, which will be uninteresting for that very reason. In the psychophysiological phenomenon that we call performance, 'error' is an interesting factor because it always takes a different form.

CHAPTER XI
REASONS FOR CONDUCTING

CD: The year of *Le Marteau sans Maître*, as you have just said, was also the year in which the *Domaine musical* began. It was then that you came into contact with instrumentalists who played contemporary music, but with very few conductors capable of directing it. So, by force of circumstance, you became a conductor. No doubt your work with Barrault had already given you some experience?

PB: My experience was not very extensive. The music I had conducted for Barrault was not very difficult, but it had certainly taught me the rudiments of the job. When I became involved with the organisation of the *Domaine musical* I found, in fact, very few conductors who were both really competent and above all prepared to undertake such a risky venture. The first concert of the *Domaine* was conducted by Scherchen, who must be mentioned first and foremost. He was one of the very few who could conduct certain music of the recent past (Schoenberg, in particular) in a competent way, and he was also one of the few who were willing to risk playing new scores. Rosbaud, too, whom I had invited to bring his Südwestfunk orchestra, was one of the great contemporary music specialists at that time. But apart from these two there was practically no one. What is quite extraordinary is that both Rosbaud and Scherchen were about sixty years old at the time – Scherchen was actually older – so that I was, not panic-stricken, but somewhat surprised that I could only count on people thirty years older than myself for professional help. I decided then that what our generation needed was to be able to acquire a sufficiently high level of professionalism to do justice to this music, which was our own, and to present it in the best possible conditions. That is how I gradually came to conduct, out of necessity, because if you write works and want to have them performed you must be able to do it independently. You can't keep calling on two or three indispensable people. Moreover, the very idea of being indispensable is one that I have always utterly rejected. If you are confronted with a situation in which you must act, you must take a decision and do things in such a way that it becomes possible to act. That is what led me not only to conduct myself but also to organise these concerts.

At that time the *Domaine musical* brought me more worry than anything else. In Paris in those days contemporary music was always spoken of derogatively without anyone having heard it. There was a kind of ruling class of conductors who refused to be interested in what we were doing. If they occasionally suggested that they might put on a work it was a great favour, much as they might give a crust of bread to a beggar. I did not find this a very encouraging attitude on the part of the 'conductors in power', but we had to get out of the stagnation and show that we too were capable of organising and performing concerts of the music we had at heart. Ten years later I published the *Domaine musical's* record[20] : for the recent past alone — and I am referring in particular to the three Viennese — the *Domaine musical* virtually brought to light between fifty and sixty per cent of their compositions between 1954 and 1964 — many years after they had been written. It was in 1957[21] that Rosbaud came with the Südwestfunk orchestra to give the first Paris performance of Alban Berg's Three Orchestral Pieces op. 6, written in 1914. For forty-three years no one in Paris had thought of performing them. Not only this, but from 1945 to 1957 there were twelve years of musical activity during which Berg's was a recognised name, but even then no one, not a single soul, had taken the trouble to perform these Three Orchestral Pieces in public in Paris. That is aberration on a monumental scale.

CD: Would you not say that at that time your work as a conductor, and the exemplary nature of its success, contributed a great deal towards rescuing contemporary music from its embattled position? Wasn't it through your conviction and accessibility as a conductor that the public came to accept music to which it had previously been indifferent?

PB: Up to that time, in Paris at any rate, performances of contemporary music had always been in the hands of extremely incompetent people. I cannot name names, but you know them as well as I do. There was a lot of goodwill, devotion even, but the lack of competence was really striking and distressing. I can remember hearing certain performances, for instance of Schoenberg's First Chamber Symphony — not, after all, a problematical work — or of Berg's Chamber Concerto, that were so incoherent, so utterly inadequate, and in which the tempi were taken at such an inappropriately slow pace that I can quite see why the public had their doubts about the music. In fact I felt the same when I heard some of these concerts. I knew the works from the scores, which I had read, and when I suddenly heard them performed in this way I wondered whether I was not perhaps suffering from some sort of aural squint: when I read the scores I heard the works in a certain way and found them both valid and valuable, and then suddenly, at these concerts, I found myself thinking that these scores could not possibly contain any musical substance of interest. I would then return to the music, and finally convince myself that the score was right after all; I could see the reasons for my own disappointment, but performances of this type discouraged a lot of people from ever again submitting themselves to other experiences of the same kind.

What was so pitiful with contemporary music at the start, and above all with the music of the Viennese, was the lack of complete professionalism. Enlarging the problem, that is why I adopted the position I now hold. Perhaps this is an obsession with me, but if you have to be professional you might as well strive to be the best, and if you have any gifts you must work sufficiently hard to be genuinely in the first rank and to give really good performances: you are then much more at ease with yourself. As long as one has not completely mastered professional standards, contemporary music will be a kind of minor specialisation that is always suspect. You can only get it accepted if you yourself are regarded as being professionally reliable. If you have been seen working on other music in which everyone knows that you cannot cheat, people — and not just the public, but musicians too — will feel confidence in you. It is in the realm of professional high standards that I have largely contributed to contemporary music. The *Domaine musical* was an experiment in which works were rehearsed with a maximum of care. Very few of these concerts — and I still remember them — were spoiled by deficiencies in rehearsal. It did happen, of course: over a period of twelve years it is inevitable that sometimes the level of performance will fall short of the level of intentions, but in the majority of cases we achieved everything we possibly could. This preoccupation with quality brought us a loyal public. If you went to the *Domaine* you knew that you might wonder about the works you heard, you might question their merits – and people did not fail to do so, even vocally and fairly loudly on certain occasions – but there was never any doubt that a work would be interesting to hear, because you could be virtually certain that it would be presented to the best of our abilities. That is probably what broke the ice, and that is why in the end contemporary music became no longer a matter reserved for tiny groups of specialists but was expanded to people who were curious about it and could feel confidence about its presentation.

CD: The critics were won over. And in every country this music passed into the network of commercial distribution. In Marxist terms one might say that to this extent it became reified. Would you say that art can be more productive when it becomes a part of the commercial network and is no longer in an embattled position, than when it is fighting in the underground?

PB: The fight is by no means over. If you look at official forms of musical activity and their programmes you will see that progress has hardly been immense, and by far the majority, if not ninety per cent, of musical life is still much more concerned with the past than with the present. There is, as you have said, a present-day circuit on a commercial basis, but 'commercial' is rather a big word to describe the contemporary-music circuit. There are certainly regular events in this field, with a more or less constant public, but the percentage is still a small one. One shouldn't worry about this period of reconnoitring.

In my view the problem you pose is a false one. You don't acquire worth by belonging to the 'underground'. There are a lot of failures in the underground too – people who have not mastered professional problems and have remained amateurs. They probably have some interesting ideas, but they are extremely weak when it comes to realizing them. Those people will always remain in the shadows in spite of everything; they may consider themselves victims of injustice or perhaps believe their researches are so pro-

75

found that they are beyond the reach of the public, but these are just consolations they find for themselves. Given all the openings that there are today for the performance of works, there are really no more outcast composers. Moreover I am absolutely opposed to this idea of the outcast composer: it is an idea belonging to the nineteenth century, when the social hierarchy was extremely rigid. Our own social hierarchy is sometimes so fluid that there is no need to stay in the 'underground' or in the shadow of contention. It is much more difficult to enter the system itself and try to change it from within. This has been one of my major preoccupations since 1953 and now, with organisms that are at once more official and much more effective through being official, what I am interested in is precisely this attempt to transform existing systems so that they will face the present. There is nothing reprehensible in this; quite the contrary, since what we are all aiming at is communication. You do not write a work simply for the pleasure of communicating it to a few friends and a few interested people. Even if that is interesting to begin with, there is in each of us a desire to communicate with a lot of people – we need not go into details about the number or the circumstances – there is this desire to be understood and assimilated. It is quite natural to try to change existing organisms so as to facilitate this communication.

It would not be at all natural to try to do that at all costs – in other words, to write music in terms of the public you want to convince. There one would run the risk of being merely local – in historical terms, I mean: one would convince a public in certain circumstances for a certain number of years without being able to convince it beyond that period. A valid work, on the other hand, even if it may present difficulties, will in any case establish the composer's communication with the public, even if it happens later or in different circumstances; it is written with communication in view – communication with the unknown listener. There is a story – in the Acts of the Apostles, I think – which has always impressed me: when Paul first arrives in Greece he sees a temple dedicated 'to an unknown god'. The composer is in much the same situation: he dedicates his work to an unknown public – it is a gesture of communication, but communication with the unknown, with the infinite, more or less. It is quite legitimate to want to hasten this communication, and put to the test works that have

76

been composed in a particular situation, but it is also legitimate to preserve one's autonomy and an independent source of inspiration.

Now that communication between the contemporary composer and a certain limited public has become easier, many people have lapsed into facility because the conception itself is directly dependent on this kind of circuit, which you called commercial, and which I would call a circuit for the transmission of contemporary music. From this point of view it has harmed contemporary music. Weaker characters have fallen into the trap and have written their music entirely in terms of this small network. But that is a secondary problem; there will always be weaker characters ready to succumb to this temptation.

To try and counteract the effects of this network and its inherent weaknesses, what is needed now is a return to a very firm theoretical approach, an approach that has largely been abandoned for the past twenty years in favour of aesthetic criteria which have become so inflated that the very technique of composition has suffered a great deal. Over the years, more and more liberties have been taken which are no longer real liberties since they depart from no theoretical criterion. This is a real danger, not resulting from the search for communication with the general public; but communication being easily established between a small public and the composer, the latter has tended to become a purveyor for this small commercial network of transmission. He should be reminded, in my opinion, of his responsibility not only to a public, however small, but also to himself — a responsibility that should lead him to turn to an unknown public, the public of the future, infinite in scope, so that they may bear witness to this responsibility.

CD: As far as conducting is concerned you have been self-taught. Nevertheless you have known all the most important conductors who played contemporary music. You have mentioned Scherchen and Rosbaud; you knew a third, Desormières, and possibly others too. Is there anything that you have either learnt or avoided after watching these conductors?

PB: I have retained some of their methods of work, but I did not watch them for very long. I observed Desormières at work a lot at one time. The reason I did not mention him in connection with the foundation of the *Domaine musical* is that he had been ill and was almost paralysed; otherwise he would certainly have taken part. Since 1955, and particularly since I went regularly to Baden-Baden, I saw a lot of Rosbaud in rehearsals, including those of my own works. Of Scherchen I remember especially his rehearsals of *Pierrot Lunaire* and of Schoenberg's *Serenade*. But these experiences have passed into my subconscious; if I learnt anything from these conductors, it was probably of a very general kind: I should be incapable of describing in detail Rosbaud's rehearsal technique, or Scherchen's stick technique. I can remember a few points of detail – especially Rosbaud's patience when instrumentalists made mistakes. This is something I probably learnt from him, because if instrumentalists make mistakes it is not because they want to but because they don't understand or have difficulties; so you must help them to overcome them. I also remember that Scherchen was very keen on certain details of phrasing. In Schoenberg he would draw the instrumentalist's attention to the phrasing itself. This was a major preoccupation with him. But beyond these details – and I can't remember any others – I myself learnt conducting by trying out what seemed to me the best thing and becoming increasingly sensitive to the responses I got. I should find it very difficult to recall how I conducted in 1955; I have always had a good ear, so that I was aware of mistakes and would put them right. Probably I subsequently became more and more sensitive to questions of style, of phrasing, of tempo, of balance (both structural and instrumental), of timbre and of colour. A vast number of things enter into conducting, not to mention the psychological factors: when you are conducting an orchestra you have to match your approach to the temperament of the players.

At first I conducted a lot of chamber music; I was thus in direct contact with instrumentalists who were extremely keen to work with me at the *Domaine musical*. They were not unknown to me, so I did not feel obliged to show them what I was capable of. Sometimes we were all equally at sea when confronted by some particular piece of music – Webern, Nono or Stockhausen – which they were no more used to playing than I was to conducting. Thus we had virtually the same problems – problems of instrumental, technical and even aesthetic assimilation.

78

Before this time, performances of Webern — especially — had always repelled me because of lack of care in the matter of sonority. Instruments became ugly and took on an aggressive colour; there was a complete lack of continuity between the instruments, no flexibility in the structures, and no feeling of transition from one part of the work to another. I particularly remember a performance of Webern's Symphony op. 21 for two clarinets, two horns, harp and strings in 1946 when I was quite overcome by the stupidity and the 'irrelevance' of the music when interpreted in this way. One wondered why people were playing those notes when they might just as well have been playing others. The music became so *stupid* that you felt that here was an invention having nothing whatever in common with musical invention. When I myself tackled this problem I told myself that there were matters of phrasing to be considered and possibilities of a different kind of instrumental approach. I take the case of Webern because it is a very simple one. Later, when I myself first conducted *Le Marteau sans Maître*, Stockhausen's *Zeitmasse*, or other things of this kind, even from the purely mechanical point of view I naturally found instrumental difficulties of a really sizeable order as well as difficulties associated with chamber music — problems of ensemble and timing. But in Webern there are hardly any difficulties of this mechanical kind. The intervals are simple; therefore the problem lies elsewhere. You have to discover how an instrumentalist can play an isolated sound in a way that links it *intelligently* with what has gone before and what follows. You must make him understand a pointillistic phrasing, not just with his intellect but with his physical senses. So long as a player does not realise that when he has a note to play it comes to him from another instrument and passes from him to yet another, or that if he has an isolated note it has a precise role within the polyphonic texture, then he will be incapable of the concentration necessary to make his note interesting. He will then produce a note that is 'stupid', divorced from the context. This is why those earlier performances of Webern had seemed idiotic to me: the musicians did not understand their roles, they played stupidly, and this was reflected in the resulting sonority, which also became stupid. An instrumental player produces an interesting sonority when he is a part of a whole whose constituent parts he more or less consciously understands.

When it came to passing from a mechanical to an aesthetically satisfactory performance the work was extremely rewarding, not simply for me but also for the instrumentalists: we each discovered the means of converging towards a single aim. This experience has influenced me enormously, and has enabled me to discover a lot of possibilities by virtue of this reciprocity between the instrumentalist and — I wouldn't say the 'conductor', a word that I find out-of-date in many cases — but the 'co-ordinator', or, to use Mallarmé's term, the 'operator'. Basically, when you are confronted by a chamber music ensemble, at a social level there will be personal relationships with each of the players. Thus you are an 'operator' in the sense that you co-ordinate all the different personalities and communicate to them something they in turn can make use of, namely your own personality. This is sometimes an extremely subtle exchange and having experienced it, and having seen the necessity for making greater and greater differentiations in the relationships between the central operator and the personalities around him, it helped me to conceive musical styles that were completely different in the relationships between the collective and the individual. My work as a composer has been marked not only by my much increased knowledge of instrumental resources, of the relative weight of each instrument, of what is possible and what is impossible, and so on, in other words of the entire mechanics of instrumental music, but also by the fact that relationships between the individual and the collective within a group of performers are something that can be worked out in far suppler, far more effective and far more subtle ways than had been contemplated hitherto. This was the most important experience I had at that time, and I believe it has influenced all my subsequent works.

CHAPTER XII
THE CONCEPT OF MOBILITY
THE THIRD PIANO SONATA – ECLAT – DOMAINES

CD: Speaking about *Le Marteau sans Maître*, you mentioned the idea of 'local indiscipline', in other words the possibility of choice. Was it not these local indisciplines that were behind the idea of mobility which really made its first appearance in your Third Piano Sonata?

PB: A number of factors came together to persuade me to adopt mobility. Firstly, I felt that the course of a work ought to be multiple rather than simple; secondly, I found that the typographical layout of music could be renewed by the introduction of parentheses, italics, and so on; and thirdly, I wanted the performer confronted by a work to be able to find himself in a completely fresh situation every time he tackled it. It was these three considerations that persuaded me to depart completely from traditional musical structure.

CD: You gave this Third Sonata the subtitle 'Formants'. At the time I found this surprising, as I had thought of formants more as fundamental structures – that is, like the musical figures which are the primary constituents of form. How would you justify your use of the word?

PB: It relates to the whole work. The formants – that is, the different movements of this sonata – can completely change the general form of the work according to whether they are arranged in one way of another. There are two words that I use a lot: 'formant' and 'developant'. According to my concept of the formant, the form is understood as a specific fixed structure, which is, however, movable as a whole: thus the formant in itself is fixed, and as an entity it allows no intrusion into its homogeneous structure, but its place within a work may vary. Developants, on the other hand, are the interferences that may occur between musical ideas which are not homogeneous and which can cause discrepancies between the different phases of development. The published formants, moreover, are very homogeneous in their

81

configuration: there is no great disparity between their component parts; whereas in other things that I have written, where you find what I call 'developants', there is a deliberate lack of homogeneity.

CD: A moment ago you were saying that you came to feel that a work ought not to have only a single possible course. Would you say that its status really changes when it has more than one?

PB: There is no real change in the work's status. You give it a certain degree of flexibility, but that doesn't change its significance or even fundamentally alter the perception one has of it.

I have often compared a work with the street-map of a town: you don't change the map, you perceive the town as it is, but there are different ways of going through it, different ways of visiting it. I find this comparison extremely suggestive. The work is like a town or a labyrinth. A town is often a labyrinth too: when you visit it you choose your own direction and your own route; but it is obvious that to get to know the town you need an accurate map and knowledge of the traffic regulations.

Personally I have never been in favour of chance. I do not think that chance has much to contribute on its own account. So my idea is not to change the work at every turn nor to make it look like a complete novelty, but rather to change the viewpoints and perspectives from which it is seen while leaving its basic meaning unaltered.

CD: The chief visitor will obviously be the performer. Do you think that the listener will find the same advantages in this multiplicity of routes through the work?

PB: The listener will find the same advantages if he hears the work played in different ways by different performers. It is just the situation of traditional single-route music writ large. Obviously no two performers go through the same work in the same fashion. There are differences in speed, different points of view, not only on the same route but on the very idea of a route. Thus it is possible, and very interesting, to see how a performer will take his bearings from certain phenomena and bring these more into evidence than others. When I myself perform certain of my open works there are particular routes that become more familiar to me.

From a number of possibilities you select one or more belonging to the same family, or perhaps one or two that are quite opposed in character – the choice is quite a legitimate one.

From the start, people have been obsessed with the desire to show a work's mobility straight away, for example by playing it two or three times in the course of a single concert, or else playing it again after a couple of days. For me it is not important that the listener should immediately perceive the mobility of a work; what is important is that the work should have an infinite number of possibilities before it, for an indefinite period of time: in other words, it will take on a slightly different aspect each time it is heard in a different context. The interest does not lie in comparing two facets of a work but rather in knowing that it will never have a definitely fixed appearance. There is an amplification of what the work really is. A work, even with a fixed course, is nothing but a code or an appearance which one modifies and models. In mobile works, one modifies the appearance in a much more profound way.

CD: This Third Sonata has hardly ever been heard; is that because it has not yet been published in its entirety?

PB: I don't want it published because the three pieces that remain unpublished have not been completely finished yet. Two pieces have been published and a third has been begun, and has been in an advanced state for some years now; I shall now finish it before very long as I want to get it off my mind. It would not have been good to bring out these other formants, as they would no longer have borne any relation to the two formants already published. This is a work that I have changed a great deal: in the first place I conceived the formants in a fairly simple relationship to one another, but in the long run the importance assumed by the central formant has obliged me to reconsider all the others from the point of view of proportion, so that the rest of the work as I originally wrote it can no longer support comparison with the central formant.

CD: For a long time your work as a composer was accompanied by theoretical considerations, usually expounded in article form. The Third Sonata was accompanied by the article 'Aléa'[22], which was not limited, however, to setting out your position with regard to mobility and chance; it also contained a polemical section in which you violently denounced certain current ways of conceiving mobility. And here, once more, a lot of your colleagues of your own generation were very much taken aback by this fresh change of course.

PB: In many instances these abrupt changes were necessary because there had been a kind of craze against which I have always fought. One discovers something and the majority of people – not all, but the majority – plunge headlong into this new discovery without either weighing the consequences or being aware of all that is involved. It is all very well to talk about chance, but then you must consider what its intrusion into a work of art represents in general terms – and it was on this point that my article became relatively polemical – and that the aesthetic project itself can be annihilated by the admittance of pure chance. Chance, as such, is devoid of interest. It cannot be part of any aesthetic project, being quintessentially a denial of it. All it can contribute is some elements, bits and pieces, and ultimately its only interest is a statistical one – in other words the statistical chance that one in a million things may be interesting. When I am made to listen to a 'work' that has been thought up in this way, it is quite beyond me to sit through a million uninteresing events in the expectation that I might eventually hear one that is interesting. In the first place I do not have the time to spare, and in the second place I think that aesthetic choice consists precisely in retaining the one interesting thing out of the million uninteresting ones. To claim to be creating a musical 'environment' to which one need pay no attention until it becomes of greater interest is an excuse for total laziness: laziness of planning, laziness of thought, and even laziness in performance.

Attempts to use theoretical points of view to justify or to demonstrate the validity of pure chance in music hinge on sophistries that remind me of the debased period of Greek thought in which anything and everything was justified by any and every idea. Reasoning comes to nothing: phrase follows phrase, bearing no relation to anything fundamental connected with reality. When someone argues, as a justification of chance, that you cannot reject uninteresting things in case they become interesting, the sophistry becomes quite simply grotesque. At that point one must be severe towards this kind of position, which is simply an excuse to abdicate responsibility.

Conversely, I have often heard it said that the introduction of free elements in music is an abdication on the part of the composer. I believe, however, that the introduction of a dimension of freedom rather entails an increase in the composer's powers, since it is far more difficult to build a town than to build a street: a street leads from one point to another, whereas a town has lots of streets and presents many different directions for building. So I do not agree at all with this criticism: a composer does not abdicate his responsibilities when he allows his performer the freedom to choose certain routes or certain ways of interpreting his music.

But I am absolutely opposed to the abdication of the composer who introduces chance operations which have every likelihood of being uninteresting, and which moreover demolish any idea of a musical vocabulary. I cannot see why people cling to arguments which still involve an elaborate form of semantics when they apply them to 'works' in which semantics is completely ignored.

CD: Clearly Cage goes even further. According to him, his work does not even have any aesthetic postulate, and is therefore purely unaesthetic.

PB: There are some activities one ought not to want to indulge in. The unaesthetic or anti-aesthetic work — just what is it? It is the acceptance of a passive attitude towards what exists: it is an idea of surrender.

Applied to areas other than music — to the social phenomenon, for example — an 'anti-aesthetic' position might give rise, not to absurdity, but to an anti-social outcome. The anti-social overtones of such a position seem to me so obvious that at this stage you are ripe for the sort of fascist society which barely allows you a corner to play in. To my mind it is like deliberately wanting to play the court jester. It is a highly dangerous position, even from the political point of view, because a certain kind of society will accord you the privilege of being court jester on condition that you accept the position and don't try to step outside it. Now as I see it, this desire to be the court jester, the jester of society, and to give that society a pretext to be a closed society with fascist tendencies, is an altogether repulsive and abject state of mind.

85

CD: That is probably why Cage has never been able to seem a progressive figure, although he might like to have been.

Still on the subject of your article 'Aléa', I would like to introduce a less serious note by pointing out that in your writings there is always a curious difference between the language of the polemical passages and of the theoretical ones. In the polemical sections, the language tends to be distinctly more poetical, in that its syntax and rhetoric admit of what might be called leaps, both in semantics and in syntax. These are not found in expositions like, for instance, 'A la limite du pays fertile', or in any other theoretical article. Do polemics stimulate you to write poetry?

PB: I hope so. I feel the need to justify the theoretical aspect of my ideas by rejecting many other things, but this rejection after all calls for a certain sense of humour and a sense of the dimension of language: it should not only be justified theoretically, but also presented in a more striking manner than the rest. A theory can be presented in a sustained and lucid way; but in a discussion the arguments must not only be clear but they must also be striking. Naturally I have a great liking for this kind of writing.

CD: Since we have been talking about internal mobility in works, I should like to anticipate a little. I should like you to talk about the conception of mobility in the small structures of *Eclat* and *Eclat/Multiples*.

PB: In the first section the mobility is implicit. It is a sort of group where mobility rules. The nine instrumentalists depend on the conductor's wishes for co-ordination between themselves and with him, but they are completely independent in that they realize the musical figures themselves. These are written out because I believe you must provide a text for the imagination to take hold of in a confident and convincing way; but once the musicians have received the signal they are free to give their own interpretation to the small fragment. There is contrast between an obligatory and a free dimension: the obligatory dimension is the conductor's decision, and the free dimension is the manner in which the instrumentalists respond to that decision.

This process is very much amplified in the subsequent sequences, although there are completely fixed ones. Indeed, in this work I also applied the principle of total determinacy in the writing:

86

there is no ambiguity at all in the text, and I try to create both fixed single-course developments and multiple developments. In this work I reintegrate the classical approach that was customary up to our time. It can still be of use in writing for groups since the collective can express itself in a purely collective way – playing together, as an ensemble – for a certain time, and then it can break apart to find its constituent individualities. In fact, there is a spread of all the possibilities open to the collective.

CD: How do you explain the title 'Eclat'? Does it relate to this mobility, or to the events you have been talking about?

PB: 'Eclat' is a very ambiguous word. I sometimes choose titles so that they can have many meanings. First, 'éclat' means a 'fragment'. In fact the first version of Eclat is very short. Then it can also mean 'explosion' and 'reflections of light', very fleeting reflections. But all these words have different meanings which can refer to the form of the music, to its content, and to its poetic expression. I chose the word 'éclat' because of its many different meanings.

CD: In your next work, Domaines, there is a rather more unexpected form of mobility: that of the instrumentalist. The clarinettist moves about from one instrumental group to another. Is this a way of drawing him more closely into the form of what is being played at any particular moment?

PB: The course he takes is in fact the course of the music: the form, even the paper it is written on – the 'part books' – fall into six structures. The soloist thus manifests his presence in accordance with the six structures he has to play. There is no way in which one can make the structure itself more clear than by rendering it visible through the instrumentalist's movements: but this is no more than a geographical representation of what happens in the score. It could be played without moving about, but this would give a false perspective of a piece that actually has a very clear tendency to individualise its various component parts. Each 'book' corresponds to one group of instrumentalists, and when the soloist plays a book he is associated with a group.

Very soon I intend to revise Domaines because, even after re-working the score later, I am not at all satisfied with its continual alternation between the entries of the instrumentalist and those of the group playing either before or after him. Now, with the existing music, I shall integrate the soloist with the group in front of which he is playing. This will take me some time, but the musical substance is already there and all I have to do is to transform it and — I'm sorry to use this word yet again — make it proliferate in a certain direction. The structure is too simple, especially for a work of this length. What is needed is a more complex structure, and above all more ensemble work. I can now see enormous possibilities for reciprocal action within this group of twenty or so musicians, and I am keen to exploit them.

CD: Would you not say that the possible permutation of the different parts of this work is also a little on the simple side? If we come back to your idea of visiting a town, here all we should do is surely to cross through the same town again and again, simply setting off from different points?

PB: Yes, I agree: this symmetrical arrangement of visits to the instrumental groups is too audible. Even if the soloist is momentarily associated with a particular group, the other groups could still have their say and this would give perspective; that is what is lacking in the present version, which simply focuses on the soloist and the group he is visiting — the other groups are in the shadow, almost non-existent.

What is interesting — and I do not propose to dwell on this point for too long, since it is manifest in all my work — is to relate perspectives to a more central point, at the very moment of listening. Thus, in the version of *Domaines* I shall be working on, I want to try to create an interplay of perspectives in relation to the groups that are not being used. There will be just two approaches: either the total collectivity will be very important in relation to the isolated group, or else the isolated group will remain the most important, but will be surrounded by shadow and perspectives. I think this is indispensable if the piece is to have a dimension that at present it lacks.

CHAPTER XIII
THE CONCEPTION OF HARMONY
STRUCTURES II FOR TWO PIANOS

CD: Discussing the second book of *Structures* for two pianos — so different in every respect from the first — commentators have seen an affinity with Debussy. Does this affinity not exist at the poetic level rather than in any real way? Are not the two musical languages so far distant from each other that any comparison becomes impossible?

PB: Any comparison with Debussy is absolutely irrelevant: it is really quite meaningless. Occasionally there may be one or two chords suspended in high resonances: this is one element of Debussy's instrumental vocabulary that I in my turn have used, but it has nothing to do with Debussy's musical grammar, his aesthetics, or even his ideas on composition. In the second book of *Structures,* and especially in the second chapter, I investigated the possibilities of the independence of the two pianists, and in particular the sonorities available on the two pianos, and this has influenced many other composers: piano writing — especially two-piano writing — has not been the same since the second book of *Structures.*

I had already conducted many investigations in the field of piano sonorities with my Third Sonata, particularly in its central formant. In general the piano is an instrument that is mainly used in its middle registers, and is only used in the extreme registers as a secondary feature. In the first book of *Structures* I used the entire keyboard, but in the second I wanted to define specific areas of sonority and to create sonorities that would be as striking as possible in individualised registers using small sections of the keyboard: one piano keeps to a central register whilst the other zigzags from one register to another; there are long stretches in the high registers and long stretches in the low. It is fairly striking to hear sonorities that are extremely contrasted and sometimes also close together, as well as the whole interplay and reciprocity between the players. What interested me was to bring into relief the soloists' dependence on each other in the matter of pianistic invention; I find the work quite satisfying from that point of view.

CD: One line of investigation, which doubtless took root in *Le Marteau sans Maître*, but which seems to me most evident in the Third Sonata and this second volume of *Structures*, concerns harmony which, at that time, was particularly localised in what you call 'frequency bands'; and this has given rise to the phenomenon of 'frequency multiplication'[23].

PB: What worried me increasingly in my own early works and, for instance, in the works of Schoenberg was the absence of control over vertical structure. Harmonic encounters took place more or less by accident. Melodic lines had reached an extreme degree of refinement, but side by side with them were harmonic relationships that not only lacked refinement but were the result of pure chance.

It was probably Webern's Second Cantata op. 31 that pointed the way to a particular solution of the problem. The pure counterpoint he writes in the sixth movement of this work is quite admirable from the intervallic point of view as far as each individual voice is concerned, but the vertical combinations produce completely uncontrolled chords: statistically, this produces for most of the time chromatic chords, but also once or twice there are common triads and fourth-chords. To use a term borrowed from science, the 'class' of the melodic line has absolutely nothing to do with the 'class' of the harmony: the two are quite incompatible. In the fifth movement, on the other hand, the four melodic lines meet at the same point to form a specific harmony; they then break out of phase and form a counterpoint whilst still retaining the same harmonic relationship since they are derived from one and the same chord. Here the counterpoint becomes entirely convincing because the vertical, the horizontal and the diagonal aspects are controlled by the same laws.

This is what I have sought more and more, and in my most recent works practically all the pitches are deduced from each other by means of harmonic systems such as those which can be multiplied by each other. I believe it is impossible to write in two different dimensions following two different sets of rules, and that one must in fact follow laws that apply reciprocally to the horizontal and the vertical. The great advance in counterpoint in the fourteenth and fifteenth centuries was the discovery of laws of vertical control that would also respect horizontal phenomena that are governed by the same laws as the vertical ones. This is why I have often been absorbed by a concern to discover clear vertical relationships. In our perception of music, identity is not just identity of the melodic line: this can only be achieved when there is perfect agreement with the vertical relationships. One has to reach the point of being able to hear them in a completely automatic way, and to forget about them because they are so obvious; otherwise your attention is divided. If we can unite harmony with melodic line under laws common to both then we begin to find a solution that will considerably enrich the musical vocabulary.

CD: We ought, however, to say that the laws of tonal music have drawn a distinction between harmonic and melodic components; even if harmony has to a large extent governed tonal melody, their laws have remained distinct.

PB: Their laws have remained distinct, but at the same time there have been very clear common factors. For instance, a melodic line would have certain points of inflection which called for a particular harmony; and likewise, in strict counterpoint, the superposition of melodic lines had to respect a certain harmonic succession. There can be no doubt about this.

CD: What you just said puts me in mind of tonal music not only in connection with the question I asked but also because the system you call 'frequency multiplication' gives rise to forms of harmonic derivation that might be compared with those, found in tonal music, known as chordal inversions.

PB: It is this kind of phenomenon that guided me. In order to produce a standard object you must have not only the same components but also what mathematicians call a 'class of objects' answering directly to one's perception of them. This is what I have tried to do; and, in particular, I have tried to polarise certain classes of object around certain very perceptible and conspicuous centres. At the end of the first chapter of the second book of *Structures* there is such a polarisation around a B flat that is repeated three times. The entire peroration is based solely on chords and sound objects

91

pivoting round this B flat – in other words, the ear is progressively polarised by certain constants.

In the musical language of the first book of *Structures* there was no polarisation, no equilibrium: everything was in a state of constant evolution. Now, in a rather more subtle manner, I have found points where the vocabulary is in a state of evolution, points where there is sometimes a little, sometimes a lot of movement. The harmonic vocabulary, too, should obey a law of evolution rather than a statistical generalisation. The textures evolve, but the way in which they are arranged is at least as important as their density. If you write things that are extremely dense and active followed by things that are simple and rarefied, what is important is not that they are rarefied or complicated but that both can be heard from one and the same point of view. In some works where accumulations are piled up without sufficient care you realise that any accumulation at all would have produced the same result. What is needed is in fact an accumulation or a rarefaction that has a meaning, and this meaning can only be given if you pay extremely close attention to the vertical aspect.

CHAPTER XIV
FURTHER CONVERGENCES WITH POETRY

CD: Following the chronology of your works we now come to
Pli selon Pli. Of this work it can be said that its genesis was truly
open for all to observe. It was heard at different stages of its
existence: first the two *Improvisations*, then *Don* with piano,
then the third *Improvisation*, and finally all five pieces.

A lot of people, especially in literary circles, were surprised to
find you turning to Mallarmé, a poet who lived a long time ago and
whose work had attracted such musicians as Debussy and Ravel.
But for you there was no sense of 'harking back', as you had
virtually always 'lived in Mallarmé's company'; however, to explain
matters, perhaps you would define the reasons, the compulsion
that led you to choose a non-contemporary poet like Mallarmé.

PB: It was not a retrogressive step — it was probably even a progressive one. In Char and in Michaux, whose works I used before
coming to *Pli selon Pli*, I found many sources of inspiration, but
they were hardly obsessed with formal preoccupations. Char's
main preoccupation is rather with the selection of an extremely
pregnant vocabulary and density of expression; with Michaux it is
the development of an extraordinarily original poetic imagery.
Syntax itself, however, the concern for form, the arrangement of
the words, their cohesion and sonority as such, are not a major
concern. What attracted me in Mallarmé, at the stage I had reached
at that time, was the extraordinary formal density of his poems.
Not only is the content truly extraordinary — the poems possess a
mythology that is very much their own — but never has the French
language been taken so far in the matter of syntax. Even after
Mallarmé, and even at the same time (one might claim, for instance, that in some respects Rimbaud possessed more 'illumination', as it were, than Mallarmé), language has never been worked
and forged in the same way. Mallarmé tried to rethink the foundations of French grammar. He showed this in his poems in an exceptionally condensed manner. Even his prose writings, which are
less condensed in style, and even his lectures bear the imprint of

this obsession with reconstructing the French language with a slightly different syntax. This is what influenced me most in Mallarmé. I know that there is a certain preciousness that belongs to the fin-de-siècle outlook — I am very aware of it — but I also know that work on language has probably never been taken so far in French.

What interested me was the idea of finding a musical equivalent, both poetic and formal, to Mallarmé's poetry. This is why I chose very strict forms from Mallarmé in order to graft on to them a proliferation of music sprouting from an equally strict form; this enabled me to transcribe into musical terms forms that I had never thought of and which are derived from the literary forms he himself used.

CD: You have often spoken of this search for equivalent forms. Given the specific differences between the two languages, it might well be asked at what level they converge, if at all.

PB: There are various levels of convergence. The simplest and most emotional is the poetic one which I tried to achieve by using certain equivalent sonorities. Thus when Mallarmé uses words like 'green', 'white', 'absence', and so on, there is after all a certain sonority in music that is directly associated with such ideas — for instance, certain extremely long-held, extremely tense sounds, which form part of this sort of universe that is not so much frozen as extraordinarily 'vitrified'. It was this emotional, direct level that made me select certain poems rather than others. It was not simply because he wrote sonnets that I chose Mallarmé's poetry, but because it had a very precise meaning for me.

A further level of correspondence lies in the construction of the poem. The sonnet is a very strict construction as far as its rhyme is concerned, and implies a particular structure for the music. For instance, for one masculine or feminine rhyme I use a certain type of structure; for another masculine or feminine rhyme I use a closely related but different structure. So these *Improvisations* become an analysis of the sonnet structure, in a more and more detailed and more and more profound way. This is why I called them *Improvisations I, II, III*. The first takes a sonnet and uncovers only its strophic character, which is not very intense work; the second is elaborated at the level of the line and verse itself – in other words, it is already an analysis of the stanza; the third proceeds in the sense that the line itself has a particular structure in terms of its position within the sonnet.

I also made use of numerical relationships. There is a sonnet in lines of eight syllables, and, for instance, in a whole section of the second *Improvisation*, where the vocal line itself is at once syllabic and melismatic around a given note, the structure rests on the figure eight: in other words, all the important and most audible events relating to the enunciation of the verse itself have as their basis the figure eight, since the initial sonorities are eight in number. The very numerical structure of the sonnet served as a basis for the musical structure. Thus there is a kind of total osmosis, ranging from the poetics itself to Mallarmé's choice of numerical values in his poem. I use the word 'osmosis', but there is also a complete transformation of such a profound nature that I was obliged to produce a work and a form that were entirely original. This is why I borrowed an expression from Michaux to say that at that moment the poem was both 'centre and absence of the music'.

CD: In your conversations with Goléa referring to *Pli selon Pli*[24], the critic, as one might have expected, immediately refers to the Mallarmé settings by Debussy and Ravel. He quotes you as saying that you studied these works a great deal at the time and admit that there are certain points of comparison with your own work. Personally I have never been able to see them.

PB: It is true that I did study these works a great deal at the time, but there is no point of comparison. Not only is there no question of imitation, but neither is there the same point of view about the relationship of music to the poems. I am extremely fond of Debussy's *Three Poems of Mallarmé,* but it is probably not one of the works that had much influence on me.

CD: With Debussy and Ravel there was a search for an atmospheric, a poetic correspondence, but there was not this attempt at structural correlation between music and text that was your preoccupation.

PB: No, there was nothing of this at all. As a matter of fact the

Debussy setting that I like the best is the third, 'Eventail'. This is the one I find the most evanescent, but that is simply a personal preference and it has nothing whatever to do with the researches I myself carried out later. Furthermore, people have very much exaggerated this influence of Debussy. Obviously, since after Schoenberg people noticed a different aesthetic, they related it to Debussy. In a way it is logical, but these references should not be exaggerated; references to Debussy in my music are of a very abstract nature anyway. What is interesting from my point of view is not to absorb influences directly but to abstract them from the music and use them as such. What interested me in Debussy was not his vocabulary itself but its flexibility, a certain immediacy of invention, and precisely the local indiscipline in relation to the overall discipline. These things will not be found at all in the form of a vocabulary, but as extremely abstract ideas. It is a fact that occasionally there may be references to Debussy's sound-world, as for example in certain ways of conceiving refinements of instrumentation, but there is certainly no major direct influence.

CD: I have always felt that this attempt to relate you to Debussy was a sign of chauvinism in French commentators. Have you noticed any comparable attempts in Germany or elsewhere?

PB: When one is abroad, one is always a Frenchman, and the only name you can refer to being Debussy, then Debussy is mentioned. But he is mentioned less and less, because there are fewer and fewer reasons to do so. For instance, when you hear the longer version of *Eclat/Multiples*, it is very difficult to cite Debussy: some of the passages have nothing at all to do with Debussy's sonorities.

CD: Let us pass on to a more recent work, *Cummings ist der Dichter*. Your choice of Cummings is something new. In general you remain very faithful to your chosen few, and this is a name you had not talked about in the past. I imagine that what attracted you to Cummings was the formal play his poetry makes of internal reiterations.

PB: Sometimes I take quite a long time before making up my mind. I got to know the poetry of Cummings in 1952 through Cage. We visited a bookshop in New York together, and I asked him who the interesting poets were; he replied, 'Take that one', showing me a collection of poems by Cummings. I read them and was enormously impressed. I even gave it to a French composer, who has since given up writing music. At that time he had started a work on poems by Cummings.

I at once felt that I had a pretty direct relationship with the poetry of Cummings, but I did not feel sufficiently well acquainted with the English language to tackle one of his poems. I know my own language well, but I was afraid to tackle a foreign language. For five or six years now I have lived a lot both in England and in the United States, and have been able to get to know the language; so now I have fewer fears about tackling a poem in English. Moreover Cummings goes further than Mallarmé: Mallarmé arranged his words in a new way and tried to find new syntactical ways of combining them, but Cummings enters into the vocabulary itself, and especially in some of his poems makes marvellous use of double meanings, and of ambiguities between words. He also uses the parenthesis with quite superb mastery. You may say that it seems difficult to use parentheses in music, since they cannot be heard, but what interests me is not to transcribe Cummings's discoveries literally into music, but to find a transcription of his world in my own. These poems helped me a great deal in rediscovering a certain freshness.

CD: You say that Cummings goes further than Mallarmé. Yet, from what I know of him, he seems to be less complex.

PB: He *is* less complex, certainly. He does not go further into the poetic universe, but only into the question of intruding into the vocabulary itself. Otherwise, the poems of Cummings, when compared with a poem like *Le Coup de Dés*, for instance, are relatively simple.

CD: The word-play is at any rate clearer, and in speaking of Cummings you could hardly refer to a certain obscurity, as so many professors have done in discussing Mallarmé.

PB: In Mallarmé there is a deliberate obscurity because of the difficulty of the syntax.

CD: But since with this composition you intended to move into the Anglo-Saxon world, why do the German words 'ist der Dichter' appear in the title?

97

PB: I could not find a title for the work. It was due for performance, first at Ulm and then at Stuttgart, and I was asked for
the title so that the programmes could be printed well in advance.
In a letter in German — and as far as I can remember, my German
was probably not very good — I wrote 'I have not yet found a
title for the work but all that I can tell you now is that Cummings
is the poet I have chosen'. I then got a reply from a secretary who
had obviously misunderstood my letter: 'As for your work
"Cummings is the poet. . ", in German, "Cummings ist der
Dichter . .". I felt there could not possibly be a better title than
that, which had come about completely by accident.

CHAPTER XV
NEW FORMAL AND ORCHESTRAL PERSPECTIVES
FIGURES, DOUBLES, PRISMES

CD: Now I would like to ask you to talk about *Figures, Doubles, Prismes*, a work we have known in various different forms, dating from 1958, 1964 and 1968. This gradual genesis is worth emphasising, as there is such a difference between the section added in 1968 and the one of 1964 that for me it almost corresponds to a kind of 'time lost' and 'time regained'. Many critics have spoken of Berg and others of Mahler in connection with this added part, and I would say this is perhaps not unreasonable. I should like to know your views on the contrast between the two parts of the work.

PB: There is certainly a deliberate tribute to Berg, and in particular to that part of the Violin Concerto in which the soloist, introducing the melodic line, progressively infects all the violins with it before it narrows down and comes back to the soloist; it is a dramatic device that greatly impressed me when I conducted the work. Starting from this, I wrote a kind of large melodic line that spreads through all the violins and then comes back to its point of origin. It is a deliberate and not an unconscious gesture of homage. This is what lies at the origin of the slow section, although it has other characteristics too, but it remains quite clearly devoted to Berg.

CD: Are the existing sections to be followed by a further one?

PB: The work is not unfinished, but I am hoping to devise more movements for it. It is finished in that the two movements will remain what they are, but it is not finite and now that I have written a lot of music for small ensembles I should like to come back to the dimensions of the large orchestra — especially as I now feel quite capable of doing so.

CD: In *Figures, Doubles, Prismes* there are two major preoccupations. Firstly the modification of the players' positions within the orchestra, and secondly the formal aspect conveyed by the title itself. With regard to the first, orchestral stereophony, I believe that

99

what you wanted above all was that players required to perform relatively similar structures should no longer be widely separated from each other.

PB: In the first place, the geography of the orchestra as it now exists is of no further interest. This series of screens, as it were, or of different planes — strings, woodwind, brass and finally percussion — is fairly logical in that it corresponds to the instruments' volume (the quieter ones being at the front and the brass being at the back, as one would expect), but it does not allow you to weave the sound blocks together. They are separate, and as wholes they are rooted in their homogeneous ensembles, even in the case of solos, which are so called precisely because they are isolated phenomena within the ensemble.

This orchestral structure, this succession of immovable planes, has always worried me. In 1958, when I decided to compose this work, I thought about modifying this structure by separating the individual groups while leaving them a certain autonomy, and doing so in such a way that the woodwind in particular would be split up among different groups, and the same with the brass. The advantage of such a scheme was first to split the wind instruments from their homogeneous grouping, and then to produce effects of movement and combination in different corners of the platform, the combination coming not simply from an overall perception. I shall still keep this scheme if I add to the work since it gives good results from the point of view of sonority. When you hear the work live, the sonorities are extremely homgeneous yet at the same time scattered, so that it is not a homogeneity of neighbouring groups but a homogeneity of fusion. To that extent this new geography of the orchestra has been a success. It only presents problems for concert-giving, since the whole layout has to be changed. It is not just a matter of chairs and desks but, as I later found out, there was a problem for the players too. Instrumentalists are always reluctant to change their place in the orchestra; at first I thought it was laziness or a desire to stay close to their friends and their usual neighbours, but there is something else involved. The musician suddenly has such a different aural perspective of the orchestra that he is thrown. Perhaps it is rather curious but an orchestral player comes to feel at home in his place in the orchestra, and to form his own assessment of the sonority of the ensemble in which he has to join. If he is moved into different surroundings, and into a very different position, he can no longer hear his neighbours, or even himself, in the same way: so it has an influence on the way he plays, and he will feel that he is in an unfair position and will not be at ease. It is as if you were suddenly looking down from a helicopter on to a familiar landscape you see every day from your window. There is a very well-known passage describing this in *L'Espoir* by my great friend Malraux. A peasant is denouncing General Franco's troops and seeks out the Republicans to tell them to try to track down the Nationalists at a place he will show them. He is asked if he is certain of his information; yes, as a peasant he has known that part of the country for a long time. He is taken up in an aeroplane to locate the Nationalists' position, but now he is completely lost since from the aeroplane he cannot recognise the terrain that he has been familiar with for so many years. He is so afraid of being taken for a spy or someone who gives misleading information that he breaks out in a cold sweat; finally, by dint of concentration, he does recognise the countryside. I think that something of the same kind happens to the orchestral musician. It is a phenomenon one has to take into account. That is why it is preferable, if possible, to compose works that will last an entire concert, or at least half of it, so that the performers get used to being placed within a given sonority.

CD: I don't think it was the same kind of preoccupation that you had in *Figures, Doubles, Prismes* that caused you to change the position of the players for Webern's Symphony. Here, I believe, it was more a concern to throw the form of the work into relief.

PB: Yes, that is what it was. In this Symphony, Webern's writing is so rich that his canonic and mirror structures can be totally lost in ambiguity. For example, when a single instrument takes part in two structures, it is very difficult to produce one note with one intention and another note with a different one; no matter how refined the playing, the result will get no further than intention. I tried to make this doubly-canonic structure reverberate by multiplying the groups by four; in other words, the structure being a quadruple canon, I tried to transpose the quadruple canon into very specific geographical norms, since what also interested me was making the polyphony more audible.

101

CD: Would you say this was an advisable experiment?

PB: I think so, but only in a good performance, which is unfortunately something I have never yet had with this piece. If I played it again now, I believe we could have both a good performance and a clearer idea of the polyphony. But it is very difficult, because the players have even fewer notes to play than in the original: it is therefore much more difficult for them to 'find their place' in the polyphony, but it is still possible to do it.

CD: Given the absence of density in Webern's music, would it not be preferable to repeat the experiment on a single platform, but a very small one?

PB: No. On the contrary, I think the more it is spaced out, the better.

CD: I have the feeling that the void which is in the very essence of this score might, if accentuated, reproduce that kind of 'imbecility' of sound you referred to in connection with poor conductors.

PB: I am sure this is a difficulty, but if one has too small a distance then why have these four groups? Perhaps there was too great a distance at the performance you heard: for me, an ideal spacing would be about three or four yards between the groups — no more than that.

CD: Let us now come to the second point: the form. Is not the title *Figures, Doubles, Prismes* in fact simply an alternative for the word 'variations'? Is not the variation a presentation of figures that contain recurrent features and, being transformed in different ways, can suggest the image of a prism?

PB: Certainly it is a title for 'variations', but it implies that the work does not use 'variation form'. I avoid words that have such a precise meaning: 'variation' suggests a series of separate variations. In Schoenberg's Variations for orchestra, there are separate little segments of music in which one finds a particularly thorough form of variation. Webern's Orchestral Variations are already a lot more advanced in having an elaborate overall structure. Schoenberg's structures are really separate structures that are juxtaposed; in Webern they are not juxtaposed but interwoven, and there are

102

correspondences between them, even though here too the variations are presented in segments. What I specifically wanted to avoid in *Figures, Doubles, Prismes* was this separation of variations under different chapter headings. For me there is a perpetual variation at work in the form — in other words, figures and their doubles can make their appearance at certain moments and prisms at others, but the threads of these three aspects of a single reality are constantly present: the figure, which is the origin; the double, which can simply be a variation; and the prism, which is the mutual interaction of the figures.

CD: In speaking of variations, I was not referring to thematic variations — what Vincent d'Indy called the variation proper — but rather to the technique of composition in which musical figures are transformed.

PB: Yes. But the connotations of the word are too precise and I prefer to think of new words, or to give words a meaning that they have lost. Not to use the word variation as such is justified, because the form itself has very little in common with variation form. Sometimes the variations might just as well be called tropes: so why use the word 'variation' if the variation itself is not exactly a variation?

CHAPTER XVI
THE EXTENSION OF THE CONCEPT OF CHAMBER MUSIC
. . . EXPLOSANTE-FIXE . . .

CD: Your most recent work, . . . *explosante-fixe* . . . , seems to have passed through several distinct stages of creation.

PB: First of all, it was a text to serve as a basis for proliferation that was published in an English musical journal, *Tempo*[25] , as a tribute to Stravinsky after his death. I gave four or five pages of explanation for a do-it-yourself realization of the piece. But, as is often the way, I was asked to prepare a realization myself; and when I tried simply to use my text and the formulae I had given I found myself compelled to enrich it, so that my version is infinitely more complex than the text which I sent to the journal. This is quite normal where the process of evolution is at work.

CD: As I see it, two essential features dominate the work: a renewal of the concept of chamber music, and a fresh justification for the inclusion of the electronic element.

PB: The conception of *Explosante* is a conception I have of chamber music. What is essential in chamber music is the fact that the instrumental players are geographically brought close together in the most formal of ways and constitute a tiny society within a few square yards. This proximity produces an immediate cohesion. I have moved completely away from this conception in *Explosante*. This was already fairly evident in *Domaines*, but less so since there it was more a question of reconsidering the idea of the concerto.

Here there are eight performers, two of whom make up a pair – the harp and the vibraphone – so that there are seven parts. So, ignoring the traditional idea of chamber music in which the players are brought close together, I have here separated them from one another. They occupy the entire stage and each has an individual score whose form is that of permutation at its most elaborate. The material is derived from a series of cells that are constantly permutated, with variations appropriate to each instrument. Each part is related to the others, but not directly through immediate co-ordination, rather by an oblique sort of co-ordination. The elements are the same, but they are broken up and elaborated in different ways: even so, they are occasionally recognisable. There is either a superposition of all the players or just a single individual, due to the opposition between what I call the sequences themselves, which are transients, and the references to the original forms, which arrest the progress of the transients. When an instrument plays an 'original' it is either isolated, or superposed on references by others; after this the transients can be superposed. Thus there is a density across the superposition of the instruments' different courses ranging from one to eight layers, which is very irregular. So the encounter takes place not on a level of complete chance, but on one of prepared chance, and the encounter between actual sounds occurs on precisely the same plane.

The transformations of the sounds come in at the individual stage, for instance, where there is a reference played by an isolated instrument. This transformation of the sound is produced by an electro-acoustical process that is totally independent of all the rest: the sound of the instrument passes through a channel that transforms it, and it is not necessary that it should be transformed out of all recognition. On the contrary, in everything related to the original – references to the original itself – the sound is barely transformed at all, or if it is, its origin can be quite clearly identified.

In addition there are other means of communication between the instruments, although they do not communicate directly because each is in its own corner playing an individual part; it is rather the means of transformation which serves as a channel of communication. It is here that the means of transformation becomes an essential and not just an additional phenomenon. It forms part of the communication between the instrumentalists, of a kind that is absent at a direct personal level. This communication is established in two ways: either the sound is lifted from its direct source and made to move about the hall, without being transformed; or else it is transformed by another instrument. Thus there are cross-movements, one instrument influencing another, and the encounters arise through the texts which, being flexible, bring about encounters that are also flexible and can vary according to the way the two texts coincide: and all this takes place within the terms of a firmly established principle. The product of this coincidence of the two texts may be modified by a third or by the product of two others. In this way there is a transformation that does not only operate on the sound phenomenon, which would be insufficient and secondary (sometimes it even becomes irksome because you come to the point where any real musical phenomenon or absence of it is concealed). In this work I have tried to entrust to acoustical transformation the very principle of communication in chamber music where it does not exist either on the geographical or the natural level. Transformation then becomes an element in composition and its appearance is central to organisation and composition, rather than to preoccupations with sonority.

CD: . . . *explosante-fixe* . . . is dedicated to the memory of Stravinsky. Exactly how are we to take this tribute?

PB: For me it is not a message in which Stravinsky's influence on me can be seen. Stravinsky himself, when he wrote the *Symphonies of Wind Instruments* in memory of Debussy, set a similar example, for it is a work that could not be further from Debussy in terms of colour, form and musical ideas. In *Explosante* it is exactly the same. I had not the remotest thought of summing up Stravinsky's activities and reflecting them in an act of homage, or of choosing a particular aspect of Stravinsky that might have inspired me. At one time I thought of including a sort of quotation from the *Symphonies of Wind Instruments*, but all that remains of it is in an idea that came from the duo between the flute and the clarinet that is very preponderant at two places in the score. This dialogue (in Stravinsky's original between the alto flute and the basset horn) is the only thing I refer to even vaguely, and it is such a distant echo that it would be impossible to detect it without my pointing it out. One other reference is even more esoteric: the whole of the central flute part in *Explosante* (the first part around which everything else was organised, and which was written for an abstract instrument when the piece was published in *Tempo*) is organised around the note E flat, which in German is called Es – and Es (S) is the initial letter of Stravinsky's name. But here again no one would be able to discover it for themselves; moreover, it is not specially important, being simply an example of cryptographical coincidence – one of those musical cryptograms, of which you can find so many, that have no musical significance, only a personal meaning.

CD: What would your judgment on Stravinsky's work be today?

PB: The reckoning would be precisely the same as in my very much more polemical article of 1949 which I quoted before. At that time the problem interested me and seemed essential because of the venture into which Stravinsky had led a good deal of music – especially his neo-classicism and his playing with history. He was probably influenced by the French intelligentsia of the time. It is on the same level as what Valéry did with poetry, or Gide with *Perséphone*. They took Greek concepts and translated them in terms of contemporary taste. In Stravinsky there is a whole period of this sort of thing that I find quite devoid of interest. The period in Stravinsky's output that I find most important is from 1911 to 1923. I think it was in 1923 that he finished the instrumentation of *Les Noces*. Afterwards there are a few points – a a few oases – in his output: for instance, certain static passages in the third movement of the *Symphony of Psalms*.

However, after an adventure that had taken him – like Schoenberg – such a long way, there came this regression, this fear of the unknown and the desire to organise the world in a reassuring way. The same thing happened with painters too. For example, when one compares the Kandinsky of 1911, 1912 and 1913 – which was his most extraordinary period – or the Mondrian of 1914 and 1915 with the same painters from 1930 to 1940, one can see the urge towards discipline, the will to tame a world that had a dangerous tendency towards chaos, by reference to masters of the past. These composers and painters, usually wrongly, wanted to become part of history before history itself had made them part of its own process. They wanted to be both the chicken and the egg. In cases of this sort, the inevitable outcome of the fundamental irreducibility of things is that the chicken is stillborn.

CHAPTER XVII
RESEARCH BASED ON TECHNOLOGY
FROM POESIE POUR POUVOIR TO THE IRCAM

CD: Circumstances seem to be bringing you back to electronic music. For a long time *Poésie pour Pouvoir* after Michaux remained your only venture into the field. Is there any reason why we no longer hear this work? Is it because of the magnetic tape? Are you dissatisfied with the electronic music?

PB: I have preserved the orchestral part of the work in its entirety, because it was good; but I was dissatisfied with the electronic part. When you have a commission to fulfil you have to write fairly quickly: *Poésie pour Pouvoir* was begun in June 1958 for performance in October of the same year. You will gather that I was not given a lot of time to reflect either on the writing of the orchestral part or on the realization of the tape. It may not have been a gargantuan task, but it was certainly very tiring to go to the studio every morning to work on the tape and then to turn one's mind to the orchestration in the afternoon. It was unsatisfactory for a lot of reasons. Firstly I had been provisionally allotted a pretty rudimentary recording studio in Baden-Baden — they were going to see what they could manage for me later — and this prevented me from taking certain transformations of sound very far, and above all, the speed at which I had to produce the tape did not allow me to spend as much time over certain problems as I would have liked. This situation hampered me enormously; from the very start I was not pleased with my work on the tape. That is why I have consigned it to an oblivion from which I have no desire at all to rescue it.

I shall come back to it in the context of the activities I hope soon to be involved with in the electro-acoustical field. It is common knowledge that I now have a project on hand for founding a research institute in Paris, not only for electro-acoustical research but for research into everything related to music and to acoustics.

CD: What do you expect to gain from your experience at the IRCAM [Institute for Acoustic and Musical Research and Co-ordination] in the more or less long term? What gap do you hope to fill both from the point of view of basic theoretical research and from that of musical practice?

PB: Since I first tried to produce electronic works, what has struck me above all was that the studios very rapidly turned to doing odd jobs. In the early days there was a theoretical impulse at work in every studio — relatively modest in Paris, stronger in Milan and above all in Cologne — but very soon, because of the difficulties that cropped up, this impulse to tackle the problem in a very general and theoretical manner was switched to practical applications — not only incidental music, film music, or any other kind of music that would justify the running costs and economic administration of the studio, but even in the case of so-called serious composition. Faced with the difficulty of manipulating the equipment and above all with the difficulty of conceiving music in relation to it, composers gave up. They went back to extremely vague practices, just as if an instrumentalist who had started out by making sounds with a cigar box had never looked further and had tried to find new sonorities by more or less casual empirical methods. Finally, in all the studios, the procedures that were discovered were simply lumped together — there was no systematic inventory that would presuppose coherent research if only on the pragmatic level, but just procedures that came into being bit by bit as the machines themselves dictated. In fact in the studio the machinery was always diverted from its proper use. Apparatus intended in theory for measuring or other purposes was diverted from its true function to serve in the creation of do-it-yourself music. As a result, the time it took the first composers in the field to 'write' extremely short compositions (the yield would be a few seconds of music for fifteen or even thirty hours of studio time) annoyed everyone and people lost patience. If he had thirty hours of studio time in front of him the composer wanted to produce something of appropriate solidity. He worried about productivity not only for financial reasons, but also because he wanted the work to bear a reasonable relationship to the hours put in.

This attitude completely killed research. In research you can spend ten thousand hours without finding anything much, or finding only embryos, and here where the ground was totally unexplored there was a sort of paralysis in face of the void. We had left behind the idea that musical instruments have been completely catalogued and charted: even if they were used in a somewhat extravagant fashion, within the bounds of their paradoxical limits, we were still moving within a very restricted field. So, suddenly plunged into the sphere of electronics, or of *musique concrète* (a term that has lately been revived), the main cause of fright and bewilderment was this confrontation with an uncharted material that it was impossible to supervise: a completely undefined material that suggested no standard unit in time, space, or pitch. With scales, for instance, you can do anything: you don't have to organise a continuum. The same is true for timbres, which are very much more complex than was first thought. Rhythmic pulsation no longer exists: there are only values, durations, a purely objective time measured in tape-lengths. Now it is far more difficult to impart rhythmic impulses without basic pulsations or psychological time. This situation created panic: people were bewildered in face of this lack of regulations and the absence of all relation between human faculties and what the machine could do.

So gradually they came to put bits and pieces together in a way that made the human relationship much more visible: a relationship of almost animal warmth between the possibilities offered by mechanical juggling and what they themselves felt. From this moment, research was completely lost. More and more, people came to indulge in tricks comparable with trick photography in the cinema. This illusion became more and more attractive, but also more and more hollow, since its attractiveness could not hide the complete lack of reflection about the new materials that had become available. In all the works that have followed, the extension of time has taken on an increasingly exaggerated dimension in proportion to the material; more and more, immediate pleasure and satisfaction have been the primary concern instead of long-term conceptions.

That is why I personally abandoned work in this direction. I should have liked to have come back to it sooner, at the beginning of the 1960s, when the Siemens studio — which seemed to me to be on the right lines — opened in Munich; but at that time I had a greater immediate interest in another subject: the organisation of performance and of musical activities in general. I found myself far too deeply occupied with it, much more than I had at first imagined, so that I was diverted from the problem; and when I wanted to return to it nothing at all existed in a comprehensive way. There have been attempts. I am not saying that I am the first to bring things back on to a proper footing: for instance, in the United States there have been the researches of the Bell Laboratories, and of the University of Stanford, California. But they have been isolated cases — like research in the whole field of radio. There has always been research within institutions not primarily intended for it. Radio stations have conducted prestige operations so as to have electronic music studios wherever possible. But once television budgets began to be so voracious these little studios became a quite secondary concern. In other studios you are dependent on either a university, a telephone company or a general electronics organisation, that engages in research for reasons of prestige but will not channel all its energies into it: research is an 'alibi', a hobby or pastime. So it seemed to me necessary not to have to rely on institutions which have other aims in mind, other administrative principles and other commitments, even towards society. What is needed is an institution devoted exclusively to research: an institution that can act as a link between other organisations dependent on universities, commercial concerns or radio stations, and that will concentrate all its resources on a precise aim.

Above all it is team work: I think it would be quite useless to want to put it into the hands only of composers. In this respect I would compare musical research with scientific research. To have isolated individuals making scientific discoveries was still possible at the beginning of the century, and even in the 1920s, but not now: for instance, Nobel Prizes for science are virtually always awarded to a team. Even if the individual awarded the prize is more gifted than the others, he is dependent on their work for about eighty per cent of his results. In music, the composer's research — and I do not at all want to suggest that it is of the same kind as the scientist's — ought also to form part of a collective research programme. I am not saying that it is a collective research programme itself: of this I am less certain. If two, three or four composers combine their efforts it is possible to produce one particular composition, but in general, composition is still a highly individual phenomenon and is likely to remain so for a tolerably long time yet. On the other hand, the research into materials on

111

which it depends is a basically collective research. It puts me in mind of the work of an architect: the architect will sketch out a design for a building, but he depends on the calculations of engineers to find out the strength of his materials under given pressures, and so on. Thus his building is not simply an aesthetic project; nowadays, technology is of prime importance in architecture.

In setting up a musical project still more or less in the realm of the unknown the composer has to confront problems he cannot solve entirely on his own. That is why there is going to be a great deal for the new Institute to do in opening up the field of musical materials. This is now the essential problem, because materials will progressively alter musical thought. Throughout musical history, materials and thought have always evolved together: thought on its own is not enough. Musical instruments, for instance, and even vocal functions have always evolved in terms of musical material, and for a century, if not longer, there has been no development in our musical instruments, and the evolution of musical materials has hardly changed. It had achieved an optimum yield in terms of what it aimed at; but now it is stagnating. So it is essential that musical materials should once more advance in parallel with the evolution of the intellect. It is not enough to think, you must also bring something about; and it is this revolution in the realm of musical material that is the essential thing now, as far as I am concerned.

There is also at present a problem of communication. The Institute will look into this, but at a later date, for creative matters must have first priority. Communication comes when you have something to communicate; but even so, all these facilities, all these new musical means, have to be studied from the point of view of communication.

At present, in the buildings now at our disposal, communication is in general based on sociological phenomena belonging to a past era – not only with regard to society itself but also to the music that is produced. The location symbolises a relationship that has already been ailing for a long time, where indeed it has not sometimes been destroyed. For example, when one presents electronic music in a conventional hall, it is really very difficult to know how to listen properly; one sees only loudspeakers, and the lights are dimmed to produce a sort of religious atmosphere. Personally it reminds me more of a crematorium, and I always feel ill at ease. Attempts have been made to remedy this by adding instruments to electronics; and then, to compensate for the lack of richness in electronic sound, instrumental sounds have been transformed electronically. Thus all the old clichés of *musique concrète* have been resurrected, which is not the most satisfactory way forward, in my opinion, any more than pure synthetic music, which is also very little concerned with musical material itself and in general is quite content with the first solution that comes to hand. Most of these musical synthetisers have met with very rapid commercial success, but they have made so many compromises in this public use of electronics that today it is extremely difficult to adopt even a slightly more elevated point of view.

So it is now essential to bring together all the research activities scattered throughout the world. Furthermore, to bring about an evolution in musical thinking corresponding to other means of investigation, it must be brought into contact with new discoveries in linguistics, in the information field, and in general with all the new theories that have been elaborated in respect of language and the creative arts and which have barely seeped through into musical thought at all. The Institute will concern itself in an extremely practical way with means of advancing musical invention, but it will also be very much occupied with related areas, namely analysis of acoustical data and communication.

CD: Would it be correct to say that the main aim behind your decision to give top priority at IRCAM to theoretical research is that of countering an all-too-obvious pragmatism on the part of instrumentalists and of some composers – in matters concerning improvisation, for example?

PB: Instrumentalists by their education or their researches are placed in a situation of conserving or of investigating: they live by things that already exist. Properly speaking, they do not possess invention – otherwise they would be composers. There has been a lot of talk about 'improvisation', but even taken in the best sense of the word it cannot replace invention. True invention entails reflection on problems that in principle have never been posed, or at least not in a manner which is readily apparent, and reflection upon the act of creation implies an obstacle to be overcome. Instrumentalists are not superhuman, and their response to the phenomenon of invention is normally to manipulate what is stored in the memory. They recall what has already been played, to manipulate and transform it. The result is a concentration on the actual sound, but form is virtually left out of account. Improvisation, and especially improvisation in groups where there is a degree of sympathy between the individual members, always follows the same curve of invention: excitement — relaxation — excitement — relaxation. In so-called primitive societies a similar situation exists in religious ceremonies whose relatively simple form involves a building up of psychological tension followed by relaxation. There is a whipping-up of collective excitement and when the uproar reaches its peak there comes the need to release the tension, and a period of relaxation follows. This primitive and basic psychological pattern is the main constituent of collective ritual, above all when it is improvised and left to the individual temperament. Thus the only thing that emerges from improvisation left to the instrumentalist, or even to the composer if he is himself a performer, is a collective psychological test which only shows up the most basic side of the individual.

Improvisation has found its most explicit expression in various civilisations where it was associated with precise basic rules learnt over countless generations, that leave the way open for a spontaneous invention that is basically connected with gesture. Once gesture has been codified, you can have last-minute improvisation, because it is now based on something. This happens in Indian civilisations where the qualifications and regulations for improvisation are extremely strict; the same is true of Bali, where models are absolutely fixed. Improvisation is then simply a kind of variation on a basic model. In Europe up until the eighteenth century the codified laws for improvising were known, learnt and based on a language accepted by everyone. They were stereotypes of form and language that in fact allowed a great deal of spontaneous elaboration: it was an acquired skill, a truly virtuoso manipulation of musical language. But the more it went on, the more people tended to do without a language, and lapse into sentimental clichés. More and more, standardised images resulting from spontaneous reactions fell outside the scope of any language and so

114

there was an abandoning of form and of the idea of the 'arch' —
that is to say, of long stretches in terms of form. It is impossible
to see ahead and things are left until the last moment, so that
improvisation becomes more and more instantaneous. In India,
on the other hand, when you begin to improvise you have no
very clear idea of the material that will result, but you know
exactly how to begin, how to continue, and how to conclude.
Similarly, in the eighteenth century, to improvise a prelude one
knew very well which keys to go through: there was a set course
to guide the aesthetic language one produced. In our own time —
as a consequence of Romanticism — there is no set course of any
description; there is merely elaboration of and for the moment,
because the memory is put out of action by material that is
usually too rich or too complex, or simply the reference goes too
far back in time, and the memory cannot recall in detail the
material that has gone before. So the memory only comes into
play for extremely banal criteria and clichés such as, for instance,
repeated notes or notes separated by long silences, superabundant
activity in every direction or long held notes during which one is
supposed to meditate on the transformation of the sound, and so
on. One day when I was with someone with whom I had discussed
the problem, we were listening to a group improvising, and I
amused myself by describing what was going to come next; it is
very obvious. At present improvisation is a sequence of negations.
If a lot of things happen in register A, for the next few minutes A
will be avoided and we shall have B; then, after B has had its
outing, it will disappear and we shall have C instead. It is the
opposite of what happens in composition, where one combines
elements A, B and C sometimes in an extremely complex way.
But mixing is excluded by this type of instantaneous, improvisa-
tory creation, as a result neither of aesthetic nor of any other
deliberate policy but simply of inadequate memory — because the
mind is incapable of mixing certain elements.

CD: In addition to acoustical research on electronics, you also
plan to have a department of the IRCAM to investigate new ways
of handling traditional resources. What are you looking for here?

PB: I have now worked out at some length my whole philosophy
about the relation between the instrumental performer and

musical creation and invention in general. In the new Institute provision has been made for a department devoted exclusively to musical instruments. This is something I have very much wanted. There is a great deal to be done in this area, and we must especially reconsider the conception of the instrument itself in relation to its traditional use.

When a player is dissatisfied with the resources of his instrument, he tends to expand them beyond their normal capacity. There has been the same reaction in the so-called studios for electronic music or *musique concrète* where, for instance, measuring apparatus has been used for making music. The case is to some extent comparable with instruments: the peripheral effects and characteristics that the instrument-makers rejected — whether rightly or wrongly, but at least with a definite aesthetic idea in view since instruments were evolved in terms of the music that required them — are taken over and used as central characteristics. I do not believe much deep thought has gone into this attitude. It is not by bringing the periphery into the centre that you solve the problem of instruments. (It reminds me of Alphonse Allais, who wanted to move towns into the countryside.) The problem has to be tackled in a different way. Take wind instruments, for example. Here, instead of using them for the conventional kind of monodic writing for which they were made, the defects of the instruments are being used to produce chords and sounds that do not belong to the tempered scale, nor to the monodic character of the instruments. I have done this myself because, for the time being, one cannot do otherwise. But why not rethink the whole problem and reconsider their construction, taking a different principle as the basis? In this way instrument manufacture can progress and musical invention is bound up with it: for it is the latter that wants us to get away from conventional scales and reject homogeneous instruments that have only one characteristic sonority. Up to now, homogeneity and standardisation have been typical of European instruments. We reject this on account of particular features in our musical language; so rather than trying to solve this fundamental problem by the use of electronic means, we might just as well tackle it head-on and find out what can be done when instruments are no longer homogeneous, and no longer dependent on tempered scales, but are indeed capable of using a large number

116

of different scales, as and when desired. This seems to me to introduce an element of relativity within the instrument itself, whereas hitherto there has been an absolutely fixed hierarchy.

Moreover the instrumental player can take part in this creative work, first and foremost as a kind of skilled worker; for someone who does not play an instrument cannot fully understand the sort of contact a player has with his instrument. Practitioners can, even if only by accident, make discoveries that are sometimes of fundamental importance, simply by virtue of their day-to-day contact with the instrument. They make thousands of experiments, and it happens naturally that one or other is bound to be good. This is how instruments have improved over the years: there is nothing new about it. The innovation is then absorbed into theoretical invention, but the two must reflect one another: from a pragmatic point of view, instrumental invention, if it remains in its own area, cannot be collated with creative invention at a more general level; but the latter can be stimulated by a discovery and give it its true place in the dialectics of composition. Otherwise all you will get will be odds and ends of sound that may be interesting in themselves but will not contribute to any real dialectic of composition.

A long time ago, I drew attention to something that I found very striking when I was young, namely Cage's prepared piano of 1949. What interested me at the time was not the quality of the musical invention, but the use of the acoustical material, and the way in which a piano differs from a prepared piano. The piano is not particularly interesting because its sonority does not vary at all; it is precisely because it is such a homogeneous and standard instrument that it is a classical one. All the sounds are reduced to their most simple expression, and it is this that creates the neutrality of each sound in relation to another. But on a prepared piano, a note prepared in one way will always make this one sound, and another note will make a different sound. But then, instead of this element being integrated into the composition by its very neutrality, it tends to stand out from the dialectic of the composition because it has lost its neutrality and has taken on an anecdotal characteristic.

The same holds good for the percussion, which have been so misused of late: this abuse has led to precisely the same errors.

Actually, when you hear, for example, a note on a violin or on a trumpet, the sound is not especially striking; the sound of a percussion instrument, on the other hand, a cymbal, or a gong, always stands out as an individual factor. Because of this it tends to stand out from the context of the composition and to escape the dialectic because it is associated with anecdotal connotations. There is a centrifugal force in the material that is extremely difficult to avoid.

This phenomenon, which is fundamental to composition, has existed throughout the history of musical and instrumental evolution: either one aims at neutral material that can be totally amalgamated with a dialectic of composition, or else one is dealing with very precise and strongly characterised material that will have a tendency to stand out from its context. The same phenomenon exists in other civilisations: for instance, in the music of some African peoples (not the most highly-developed from the musical point of view) we find an instrument, the sanza, that has vibrating blades and a range of about an octave; the vibrating blades alone could make up a neutral universe — they form a scale that is fixed and modal, as all African scales are, and there are no elements of modulation or ambiguity. But in order to differentiate the sounds and give them extra interest because of their static nature one of the blades will be provided with a kind of mute with a bit of tar on it, so that the sound becomes extremely muffled. The next blade, on the other hand, will be equipped with a small resonant ring to produce a sort of nasal buzzing sound. So, starting off with a static scale, they try to individualise each sound as much as possible.

In that kind of musical civilisation and with an instrument of this sort, the procedure has every justification. But in our own musical civilisation it is contrary to the entire evolution of music to try to delimit an instrument within highly typical and in-dividualised characteristics, since we are moving more and more in the direction of relativity. At first there was relativity within a homogeneous area, but for the future it will be found in relative and non-homogeneous areas. Therefore, what the instrumentalist ought to be looking for now is not the extreme of peripheral possibilities of his instrument, but rather those that are neutral, non-homogeneous and relative (in the sense of 'relativity') and that are actually central to the instrument.

This is why I have entrusted this area of research at the Institute to an instrumentalist-composer: the hierarchy is fundamental. The instrumentalist alone, no matter how talented, how revolutionary, how rebellious or how radical he may be, will only think in terms of the instrument, whilst the composer will think in terms of a hierarchy which to my mind is very important — the hierarchy of composition and instrument.

CD: To revert to a less serious level, it is rather curious that electronic music, which was the immediate cause of your leaving France, should now provide the occasion for your return.

PB: That is what will happen. I am not much given to settling down in positions that have already been won. You must always keep questioning yourself. Conducting has enabled me to reach a certain standard of professionalism through which, whatever happens, new music has been promoted in a way that cannot now be reversed; I now feel that it is of more interest to try to re-channel my activities and to rethink certain theoretical problems where there are still fundamental gaps to be filled. And it seems to me vital to bring together all the scattered energies within a single organism so that music can be made to advance in a far more rapid and spectacular way.

CHAPTER XVIII
CONCLUSION

CD: I think that what emerges from your work as a whole, and also from these conversations, is an extreme loyalty to yourself and to those you have chosen. From the start, the composers you have spoken about have been those who were a constant inspiration in your progress and your activities. Once again, this shows the extreme ignorance of critics who claim that music is now in a period of such advanced post-serialism that there is no longer any grammar that can be ascribed to the serial principle; you, however, have proved yourself the most constant of musicians in this respect, and all your work has in fact been conducted within the series itself, bringing a progressive enrichment of its grammar. This is something which nowadays is generally completely forgotten by critics and commentators.

PB: There is a loyalty to oneself that is indispensable. You must not be bound by loyalties that have become academic, but if you want to progress it is useful never to forget what you have already done, since otherwise you can go round in circles or hold inconsistent views. What is of particular importance to me now — probably because of my age — is a new perspective. I feel that I need history less and less. Between the ages of twenty and thirty I paid a lot of attention to what had been done before me and even to what was being done at the same time; but the more I go on, the more I ignore other composers. I like hearing works of the past and even of the present, but it seems more and more important to plough one's own furrow. My few years as a conductor compelled me to absorb so much history that history now seems to me, if not superfluous, at least something of a weight on one's very being. In my view one should be rid of it once and for all. Many composers, even of my generation, seem obsessed with recovering certain musical languages of the past which they want to reinstate, either for poetical reasons or technical ones. I think it is because they have not experienced history enough: it fills their thoughts like a sort of burden they carry about with them because they

120

have not worked it out of their systems. I believe that we are entering on an era — and I feel very, very strongly that I myself am entering it — in which the burden of history will no longer count for anything. I may pay an occasional visit to a museum but, more and more, I am becoming absolutely keyed to the future. The phenomenon of our heritage is no longer important to me: only new categories of thought. In other areas — in the sciences, for example — one thinks according to different principles, and with different aims in view. It is impossible not to do this in music too. Linguistics have made enormous advances but musical vocabulary has not progressed in a comparable way. It is now or never if we are to rid the memory of a host of things and progress on a solid basis of theory. At present activities are somewhat disorganised, and not always very interesting. People do indeed want to do without history, but only because they have never known it. There are a lot of self-taught musicians, but self-taught by accident. What I want now is for everyone to be deliberately self-taught.

NOTES

[1] 'Incidence actuelle de Berg' in *Relevés d'Apprenti*, Paris 1966, pp. 235-40: originally published in *Polyphonie*, ii (1948).
[2] Chorale 'Es ist genug' from Cantata 60, *O Ewigkeit, du Donnerwort*.
[3] 'Schoenberg est mort' in *Relevés d'Apprenti (op. cit.)*, pp. 265-72: originally published in *The Score*, 6 (1952).
[4] 'Trajectoires — Ravel, Stravinsky, Schoenberg' in *Relevés d'Apprenti (op. cit.)*, pp. 241-64: originally published in *Contrepoint*, 6 (1949).
[5] 'Style ou Idée (Eloge de l'amnésie)' in *Musique en Jeu*, 4 (1971), pp. 5-14.
[6] Suite in C for piano, K399.
[7] *Der Spiegel*, 25 September 1967.
[8] Antoine Goléa, *Rencontres avec Pierre Boulez*, Paris 1958, pp. 82-3.
[9] Goléa, *op. cit.*, p. 99.
[10] René Char, 'Mise en Garde' from *Les Matineaux*.

'Nous avons en nous, sur notre versant tempéré, une suite de *chansons* qui nous flanquent, ailes de communication entre notre souffle reposé et nos fièvres les plus fortes. Pièces presque banales, d'un coloris clément, d'un contour arriéré, dont le tissu cependant porte une miniscule plaie. Il est loisible à chacun de fixer une origine et un terme à cette rougeur contestable.' (We have within us, on our temperate side, a series of *songs* by which we are flanked, wings by which are linked our restful breathing and mightiest fevers. They are pieces almost commonplace in character, mild in colouring, old-fashioned in outline, yet their texture bears a tiny wound. It is open to everyone to determine where this disputable sore spot begins and where it ends.)
[11] cf. Mallarmé, *Oeuvres complètes*, Paris 1945, p. 1437n, and *Correspondance*, I, Paris 1959, p. 181, on the origins of 'Don du Poème'.
[12] Proust, *La Prisonnière*, I, pp. 220-221.
[13] 'Eventuellement' in *Relevés d'Apprenti (op. cit.)*, pp. 147-82: originally published in *Revue musicale*, 212 (1952).
[14] 'Recherches maintenant' in *Relevés d'Apprenti (op. cit.)*, pp. 27-32: originally published in *Nouvelle revue française*, 23 (1954).
[15] Karlheinz Stockhausen, lecture addressed to Brussels University Institute of Sociology, March 1965.
[16] cf. note 14.
[17] 'Propositions' in *Relevés d'Apprenti (op. cit.)*, p. 74: originally published in *Polyphonie*, ii (1948).
[18] 'Son et Verbe' in *Relevés d'Apprenti (op. cit.)*, p. 62: originally published in *Cahiers Renaud-Barrault*, xxii/xxiii (1958).
[19] 'A la limite du pays fertile' in *Relevés d'Apprenti (op. cit.)*, pp. 211ff: originally published in *Die Reihe*, i (1955).

[20] 'Dix ans après: La musique et ses problèmes contemporaines' in *Cahiers Renaud-Barrault*, xli (1963), pp. 360-70.

[21] Domaine musical concerts, 1957.

[22] 'Aléa' in *Relevés d'Apprenti (op. cit.)*, pp. 41-56· originally published in *Nouvelle revue française*, 59 (1957).

[23] *Boulez on Music Today*, London 1971 (original edition Mainz 1962).

[24] Goléa, *op. cit.*, p. 251. The passage in question may be translated as follows:

Antoine Golea: Listening to your two *Improvisations* [I and II] . . one gets the impression that here you have brought about a kind of synthesis of influences; if the melodic line here shows indisputable reminiscences of Debussy, the writing for the instrumental ensemble for its part is derived from the *Trois Poèmes de Stéphane Mallarmé* by Ravel. They are not for the most part the same instruments, but in the dimension of timbre it is the same class of effects that is investigated and, I need hardly add, pursued to its extremes.

Pierre Boulez: Just so; I studied both works a great deal before embarking on my *Improvisations*. And even outside the dimension of timbres, I tried to add some kind of conscious awareness and of organisation to the sublime improvisation that is thrown into relief by the compositions of the older composers, above all those of Debussy.

[25] 'Canons and Epitaphs' in *Tempo*, 98 (1972).